The Story Weaver and other tales

The Story Weaver
and other tales

Sally Zigmond

Bridge House

British Library Cataloguing in Publication Data
A Record of this Publication is available from the British Library

ISBN 978-1-914199-54-7

This edition published 2024 by Bridge House Publishing
Manchester, England

To Nicola Slade and all my writing friends who are no longer with us

Contents

INTRODUCTION

The anthology comprises some of my favourite short stories, many published either in print magazines or online. Storytelling and the spinning and weaving of fibres to clothe people from the polar regions to the equator are bound together metaphorically: spinning a yarn, weaving a web of lies, pulling the wool over someone's eyes, warp and weft and so on. I have updated some of these stories for the 21st century. Chain smoking and overflowing ashtrays in cafes and workplaces have long gone; smoking and drinking every day mean a hefty supermarket bill nowadays, pubs are closing and coffee drinking has increased.

Sally Zigmond

THE STORY WEAVER

I first saw him as a black speck on the white plain; a man leading a starving horse, his eyes snow-blind, his cheeks sheened with fever. He came closer as I waited. He staggered and fell at my feet.

I took him into my tent and made him drink the blood left over from a still-born foal. He drank it without knowing what he drank. He slept for three days. When I told him what saved him, he wept. I do not know why.

When the others first saw him, they wanted to kill him. I stood before them and proclaimed him mine and they would touch him at their peril. Grins were exchanged. For it is known that I have never had a man.

He remains with us still; a man among women. He shrank into the shadows when the others were here but now they are gone. Left behind are the toothless grandmothers, the children who are weaned from the breast and me.

And the man.

We sit with the fire between us. He is always cold although the fire burns hot. I weave and he talks.

He is a strange man. He is tall but has no body hair. His skin is pale gold and his hair is black. He speaks softly. The men of our tribe are stocky with beards and hair of flame. They swagger, bone daggers at their waists. They are hunters and tamers of horses.

'Your men are savage brutes,' he says, although he has not yet seen them. 'We live in cities. We have streets, laws and good government.'

'I do not know those words,' I say. He stands up and walks to the entrance of the tent and lifts the cloth.

I hear the hobbled horses strike the ground with their hooves. It rings like hammer on metal. The wind whistles through their tangled manes. The dogs by the fire grumble in their sleep. He drops the curtain I wove three summers ago. He returns to hug the fire. Then he laughs and picks a piece of flesh from his teeth. 'To think I am living thus,' he says.

Some days later, pounding hooves, jingling harnesses and shrill cries announce the return of the women once again. The raw air is slashed by the heat of fresh blood. A hog, thin but with meat enough upon its bones, is dropped at my feet. The dogs that returned with the hunters greet those left behind with furious barks, jumping at each other's throats, tails thrashing like sword blades. The babies and toddlers wake in their woven cribs and howl. We all share the same hunger. Even the stranger.

As I put pots to heat on the fire, Olgatha enters. She helps me skin the beast and scrape it clean of flesh and fat. We throw the meat into the pots. Beneath her tunic, her new-born son suckles from her swollen breast. We work swiftly. I see the man watching her.

She was once Takalam's woman. But she is good to me.

Soon the pig-flesh has devoured our hunger. Outside, the wind screams across the plain, kicking up a blizzard. The children ask for the tale of the Raven and the Foal, but I am shy in the presence of a stranger.

He lifts his head at my words. 'In our land women do not tell tales. It is men who sing their songs to the trill of the lyre.'

'What do your women do?'

'They make themselves beautiful,' he says. 'For men.'

Does he mock me? Despise my ugliness? I feel his eyes rake my misshapen jaw and twisted back and I want to cry.

He touches my hand. 'I would like to hear your stories.'

The other women have already left the tent and returned to theirs, scooping up the sleeping children under their arms. We are alone. I reach for my knife I use to sever the yarn and the cord that binds the newborn to their mothers. 'No stranger steals the stories from our ancestors. I will not tell you.'

The night passes with no word between us. The wind drops and the tent sighs and stiffens with ice. The fire burns low. I concentrate on my loom, keeping count of the warp threads, changing the colours, the twisting of the weft beneath and over the warp. Which is he and which is I?

'Where are the men?' he asks the following day.

'Away.' I do not wish to think of the men.

'Why are they not here to take care of their women and children? Provide for them?'

'Women do not need men.'

Just then, one of Olgatha's tall daughters enters the tent and shyly hands me a skein of thread she has spun herself. I inspect it thoroughly for knots and burrs. I find none. She goes away, her braided head tilted with pride.

'If men and women live apart, where do the young come from?'

I have to explain the simplest things. 'The men come every second full moon. When they come they take away the boys who have grown beards and plant their seed within us, then leave. It is the custom.'

'But what of love?' he whispers. He is a strange man.

Now the days and nights stand as equals. Soon the days will begin to nibble the tails of the night and grow longer before the nights exact their revenge, as the old tales tell us. The grass grows again. Today I freed the horses from their ropes. They careered across the plain, rolling over and over, kicking up their back legs and playing the fool. They soon settle, their shaggy necks curved to crop the first sweet shoots of the season. Their tails flick. The flies are waking too and cloud their heads. The whole world is yawning. The sky is the colour of skimmed milk thawing in the bowl.

The moon is full tonight. Tonight the men will come. The children are excited, especially the boys. They squabble and the women cuff them about their ears. Those who will leave with them on the morrow strut like warlords.

I lift the entrance cloth. The sun stabs the floor and slices the body of the stranger who has just risen from his sleep. His back is to me. He lifts a bowl of mare's milk from the fire and places it on the rug-strewn floor. He takes a piece of foal-skin, swishes it in the steaming liquid, squeezes out the excess moisture and applies it to his body. Then he dips his face in the now cool liquid and splashes it about his face before applying a sharp blade to his cheeks. I have touched this blade. It is sharp and cold beneath my finger. When he has finished he puts the used milk to one side. He has learned that we waste nothing. The children will use it to make supple the saddles and soak the read stems ready to fashion into arrow shafts.

It is strange to me, this desire to remove the signs of manhood. A beard divides the man from the boy. His people must remain as children until they die. And yet he tells me how the call to manhood is strong in his land. He tells me that when the sun blazes fiercely above their heads they engage in vigorous sports, testing each other's strength to the very limits of endurance: running, wrestling, throwing wooden spears and discs of stone.

And now he stands up and turns to face me. The shaft of sunlight ripples across his nakedness. For a moment we gaze upon each other in wonder. I now see the beauty of the clean, white, male form. He is less thin than he was when he arrived and his muscles are well-formed. I see each sinew beneath the skin. He only shaves his face and head.

There is a straggle of hair on his chest and his cock stirs within a nest of black curls.

He is without his beard but a man for all that.

He binds a piece of cloth about his waist and strides from the tent on sturdy legs, passing close to me as he does. He smells of the spring sky and fresh grass. I watch him go. Slowly at first, as if testing his muscles, he begins to run, picking up speed, bearing down upon the group of horses. They scatter whinnying in alarm, tossing their heads, their hooves pounding the plain, before regrouping and continuing to graze.

I am used to solitude. But I have never felt lonely until this moment.

The other women are dressing their hair in tight braids, twisting strings of wool around them. They are laughing, showing their fine pointed teeth. They take it in turns to drag bone combs through the tangled flames of their hair.

I take no part in this but continue at my loom, thinking about the stories I will tell during the feast tonight. The stranger is returned. He squats beside me, shooting a quiverful of questions about what happens when the men come.

'What do you think happens when men meet women?' I laugh and am surprised by my own bitterness. I stand back and regard the cloth stretched across my loom. That at least is fruitful. The stranger has said much about the strange land in which he lives. There are beasts with skins of leather like the snake but walk on four legs. There are creatures that can live in pools of water. Their skins are featherless but they fly like birds through the water, which he says is wider than the plain, which is impossible. He says horses gallop across these watery plain, wild and snarling, full white tails streaming behind them like clouds presaging a storm. Beneath them fly the water-birds in all the colours of the known world, but more dazzling, more alive.

I recreate these strange beasts and weave them into my cloth. I will tell tales of these creatures that drink nectar from heart of flowers the size of our round tents and the colour of blood. For that is what the stranger tells me. He has made my world wider and brighter. I see beyond the brown plain, further than the edges of my mind. I feel my body stretch and strengthen.

Suddenly the women leap up and the children run screaming towards the horizon.

'The men are coming,' I tell him and he too rises and makes his way to the curtain and pushes it aside.

'I see nothing,' he says.

'Look again,' I command him as I would a child. 'Do you not see the sky darken beneath the cloud of dust that rolls towards us? How in the name of our ancestors do you defend yourselves? Do you lie down and offer your necks like curs?

I know my words have stung him. I wish they had not but I am sharp because the men have come. I have never heeded their indifference to me nor longed for their fierce embraces, but today I feel bereft, jealous of the rough attention that will be denied me. My thoughts are as tangled as raw yarn and I sense something of the excitement the other women feel and thought would never be a part of me.

The stranger too is as tense as a strained bow before the arrow flies. I see a vein in his neck throb. He is right to be afraid.

The feast is over. The boys have been handed over to the care of the men and they are enjoying their first taste of fermented mare's milk. It is always a moment for laughter as they splutter and cough and then grow sleepy. The men lie with the women in their arms, slowly stroking their bodies, savouring the pleasures to come. Some couples, the eager ones, have already slipped away to other tents.

But my tent remains full. Someone mouths a tuneless song until kicked into silence. Dogs nose the rugs, seeking discarded bones and licking grease from the children's faces. Moisture glistens on the skins hanging on the walls and trickles to the floor.

One of the men calls out to me. 'Old Crone! Tell us the tale of the braggart, Vostik and how his sword was stolen as he fucked his master's wife.'

'No,' cries another. 'I want to hear of the passion of Urmlich for the queen of the Ice.'

I stand up knowing that I will have to tell them both and many more before they will let me rest.

Takalam staggers to his feet. Takalam, my twin. My womb-companion. He sways glowing in the firelight, a giant who fiery head butts against the roof. His green eyes are fixed upon the stranger, my stranger, who is looking elsewhere, gravely regarding two women who are beginning a slow, sinuous dance, weaving between the couples, placing their bare toes in the men's mouths and snatching them back before they are bitten. I should have warned him. He should not look upon them. They are Takalam's new women and Takalam is a jealous man.

We dwelled in the womb together for nine months, our bodies twisted so tightly together our mother was cut apart to give us life. Takalam was lifted out as true and strong as a mighty tree. I was peeled from around him, a weak vine, twisted and bent. Yet, we are matched. We are both proud of our skills, but he is as handsome as I am ugly. He is harsh and I am gentle. My mind is true; his is twisted. Say one word to defy him and he cuts your throat. I have seen it.

Takalam has seen. The tent falls silent, but for the snoring of the dogs and the hiss of the fire. He draws his bone-blade from his waist and points it at me.

'The cripple has not yet told us the tale of this cuckoo in our nest. Why is he here? What does he want of us?'

Sneering laughter crackles around the tent. 'Does he want to steal a woman?' he jeers. 'Does he know what to do with one?'

More laughter – dangerous low laughter.

'Does he wish for the wild Olgatha?' Takalam despises Olgatha because she would not give him a son. He aims a boot at her backside, almost knocking her into the fire. She snarls and retreats to the edge of the crowd. 'Or this one?' He pulls a woman from the floor by her braids. 'But, remember. If you take her, I will slice the head from your shoulders and feed it to the dogs!'

Thin laughter dribbles from the drunken men like piss from a frightened dog. Takalam speaks again. 'Perhaps not, eh, stranger?' Then he slaps his leather thighs and the dogs leap up barking until he roars them to silence. 'Listen. I have a better idea. Let him have my sister. No-one else wants her!

He taunts the stranger. 'Do you have a sword?'

One of his lackeys takes up the cry. 'It will be but a blade of winter grass, soft and withered!'

'Show us your reed-pipe and pipe us a tune!'

'If he can find it!'

I flash a warning glance at the stranger but I am too late. Takalam leaps on him, then his cousin Gangest, and more and more. Even some of the younger, sillier women crawl over him and claw at his garments, giggling over his bare legs, kissing his bare buttocks.

I peer between my fingers. I see Takalam seize the stranger by his ears and haul him to his feet, gasping and spluttering. His nose pours blood and his face is bruised. He is naked. Teeth marks scour his back, his legs, his arms.

He bears his humiliation with dignity.

But I am ashamed. Of my people and that I dwell among them.

I take the knife from my belt. I slice the warp threads from the top and bottom of my loom. I shake the cloth to life. It is the red of blood, woven with the fishes of the blue and green water, the dazzling white mares of the mighty ocean that is wider than the plains. It is strange. It is magnificent and my people gasp.

I take it to the man and with it clothe his naked and wounded body. Carefully, slowly I fasten shoulder and hip buckles from carved bone and take the girdle from my waist and tie it around his. My people watch. They know what it means. It is known that this prize should be Takalam's and therefore it is known that he is slandered and humiliated. Takalam's mouth hangs open like an old saddle-bag. I approach him boldly and take the sword from his belt and present it to the stranger.

'Leave us now,' I say to the stranger. 'Go home and tell your people about us. Not of Takalam. He is rabid wolf, foaming at the mouth when the moon is full. But of our land and our ways.'

He nods. 'You have taught me much,' he says. 'This garment and the giving of it tell me everything.'

'Tales are tales. Only this is true.' I place his hand on my heart.

The next morning when only I am awake, I stand on the plain and watch the sun rise. The dawn wind ripples through the grass and a tiny feather flutters to my feet. I take it back to my loom and weave it into a new story.

UNREAL CITY

'Give me your passport. You'll only lose it. Gate Twenty. Come along.'

I follow your orders as well as your woollen hat along the crowded concourse. You stop for a moment, crouch, turn, and take a picture of me. The first on the film. In case it doesn't come out. You take hostages with your camera, you know. Once you have captured someone on film, you think she is yours to develop as you will.

We arrive and go through the usual formalities. You are totally at ease. My spirit failed to keep up with the aeroplane and has been left behind on Gatwick's tarmac. The wheels of the airport bus taking us into the city hiss over the frozen slush. You take the seat in front of me. You begin your ritual. You spread out your equipment. Counting. Arranging. Lenses. Rolls of film. Three cameras. Filters. Other things I can't put a name to. You are absorbed.

I look out of the window. I am absorbent, drawing the outside in to my inside, to fit myself into this space that has no boundaries. The flat fields of dead snow a laid out corpse, the low roofed houses thickening to salt-white blocks of flats. We pass a football stadium. At least I think it's a stadium because its outer skin is encrusted with what look like match fixture lists, torn and flapping in the dank air. But through the open gates it is a busy market. People with canvas bags are scuttling past stalls of muddy carrots and fat round cabbages. They finger racks of clothing. A father hoists a child onto his shoulders and points down to our bus. The bus moves on and they fade into memory, then lost in the mist. 'There's no substance here,' I say to you. 'Nothing to catch hold of.'

'Off you go again,' you sneer, squinting through a closed lens. 'Airy-fairy.' You put the camera down. 'I'll wait. There's not enough contrast.'

‘That’s what I mean.’

‘Then why the Holy Moses didn’t you say so?’

‘I did.’

‘Not in a way normal people might understand.’

I sulk.

We see the same. We use a different language. There is another difference. You never try to get close to things. You are happy with the second-hand. I demand the real thing. The breast versus the bottle. All or nothing for me, rooting for the elusive nipple, never latching on for a good suck. To hell with that you say. Milk is milk wherever it comes from. Guess which one of us is fat on truth and who is lean and hungry?

We pass a hoarding from which the Marlborough cowboy with his white tombstone teeth and prairie-ripe hair grins down at us. What the hell is he doing in Eastern Europe? You jump up squeaking, flashing away on auto-shutter. ‘That’s more like it. I’m getting an angle. Colour, contrast, conflict. Great!’

The road is straight and fast. Beyond a lighted window a man in a string vest is pumping chest-expanders. In another a child plays a violin. A woman opens a cupboard and takes out a pan. They are this city. They make this city. I know nothing of it and never can. I am no more than a fly I see crawling up the inside of the bus’s window. There is a barrier I can see through, but not penetrate. Unreal City.

The bus lurches over a tangle of tram-points and bounces over a cobbled square coming to a halt by the sluggish brown Vltava. Two gulls catch the sun and flash like brief beads of mercury and are gone.

I have seen plenty of summer shots of Prague of glowing green domes topping sunlit towers of baroque extravagance. Today they are sadly muted. Unreal City. Even the wind is frozen. Like a photograph. People walk by but they make no sound in their soft boots on the sanded snow. No clouds of vapour rise from their mouths. Their breath has been stolen.

You leap down the steps of the bus and land on the snow with a thud. Trust you to spoil the silence. 'Better get some shots in before the light goes completely,' you say, running ahead like a child let out of school.

A muffled bell somewhere in the twilight rings out twelve noon.

Immediately you are snapping away. Windows, gables, getting in peoples way, dodging the traffic. 'Wow!' you say when you spot a swan, bear or peacock carved above a door. 'Wow!' to every pastel wall or rococo roof tile. 'This is something else.'

My fingers dig into my palms. I shuffle my feet. I hate you for being direct, for not pretending to belong, for not trying to assimilate, for not caring how you appear to others. You crack open your crisp new map on every corner, grab the nearest person by the arm and shout, 'Do you speak English? Great. Can you tell me the way to Charles Bridge?'

You want to rush, to see everything in the guide book. But you miss things. You don't see the rolling pin arms of the woman making pastry through an open kitchen door. Two police officers bristling with firearms, their cheeks so smooth and young, who are really Hansel and Gretel, following the trail of breadcrumbs through the forest.

I have to run to keep up with you and your map. I don't want to run. I want to preserve this immobility that surrounds me. Through a bubble-glass door I see a girl. She is standing in front of a mirror drawing a comb through long, black hair. Music burbles somewhere in the background and she throws back her head and sings.

Trinket sellers jostle for space on the ancient bridge despite the intense cold. frost. Some burn tiny braziers of glowing coals. Others wear gloves as thick as boxers'. Or jump up and down.

'Plenty of colour here,' you say and again you're clicking away as happy as a hippie in a field of poppies. Not thinking about what you see. That comes later when you're in your dark-room, leaning over white dishes waiting for the pale images to emerge, ghostly at first and then square edged and substantial, something you can slice into bite-size images.

You pile your bags against the stone wall. 'Keep your eye on them while I wander about a bit,' you say and off you march, stuffing spare film into your pocket. You ignore the hawkers. You ignore everyone, except those you want to photograph and then it's 'Would you mind? A bit to the left. Look this way.' And they do it for you.

Damned if I would.

I kick my heels, looking about me. The heads and shoulders of the statues that line the bridge are hooded and caped with snow. It makes them look cute and Christmassy. Closer too, the effect is different. The black shapes are soft and sooty. Their noses are crumbling like medieval cocaine sniffers. I like the imagery. Coke and snow. It's pollution from nearby steel works that has done the damage. I stand at the foot of a black Christ crucified in a snowfield, choking on sulphur dioxide. The grieving women at his leprous toes sob into disintegrating gas-masks. I laugh at my own fancy. The cold has obviously got to my brain. I run my fingers along the black form expecting a roughness. It's smooth black ice. A moment of eternity frozen in time.

Is it possible, I muse, as I stroke the ice, to be anything but banal in this city that is steadily rubbing me out? I lean over the parapet and let myself slide along the oily blade of the river and be carried towards the grim renaissance palace that surrounds the spiky towers of St Vitus's cathedral. Christ, it's cold. Too cold to stand dreaming.

I can hear music. I disobey your orders and set off to find its source, only to find you've got there first, damn you. On a tiny canvas camping stools, like a gnome on a toadstool, sits an old man playing a series of sunny tunes on his accordion. He has a white walrus moustache and a tartan blanket tucked about his legs. He is wearing a sheepskin jacket. Old, but good. On his hands are fingerless gloves, striped like wasps. Coins rattle into a biscuit tin at his feet.

And what a smile beneath that white moustache. He is bathed in summer sunshine. He is king of the bridge, holding court on his canvas throne, guarding his biscuit tin treasury. The faces of the people passing him melt in his warmth. He knows you are taking shot after shot of him, but for once, you are not his captor. He is free. It is you who sit at his feet.

I have to break the mood. 'I hope you're going to pay him.'

'Sure I am. Oh for Christ's sake, Dee. You've gone and left five thousand dollars' worth of equipment at the other end of the bridge.'

'Sorry.'

'Is that all you can say? How can you be so stupid?'

You stomp off, muttering, to collect your gear, leaving me with the musician. He is now playing *I love Paris in the Springtime*. Perfect. The silky Seine flows beneath my feet. Chestnuts are in blossom along the bank.

I fumble in my bag for a coin. I take three and place them carefully in the biscuit tin. I can't tell from his face whether I've just given him enough to live on for a month or something not worth more than a button. When I straighten up you are pointing your camera the other way, at a brown barge chugging downstream.

There is a blind man on the other side of the bridge. I haven't seen him before although I must have walked past him at least twice. Unseen as well as unseeing. He stands like a black post, like the giant statues that dwarf him. He takes up little space. His presence is neither apologetic nor proud. He is here. He might be anywhere. But, he is here and that is all one can say about him.

Taking obscene advantage of his disability I stand in front of him. I look him over to try and make something of him. His pale white cheeks are smooth and unstubbled. An inch of frayed cord trousers hangs below a long belted coat. His shoes are suede, smoothed at the toes to shiny puddles of baldness. He wears no gloves. His hands are as raw as red meat, the fingertips as white as candle-wax.

I watch him for some time. He doesn't dance a jig to keep warm like the others. He does not blow on his hands nor keep them in his pockets. He does not beg. He does not speak. He does not smile. He does not frown.

But he wants money. Oh yes and desperately. I can sense that. There is an upturned cap at his feet. It should be keeping his head warm for all the good it's doing there. He must sense its emptiness, but his face betrays no disappointment, no anger at the silent crowds passing by. His soul is as blind as his eyes. Why is no-one giving money to this poor blind man? He is more deserving than the accordion player.

I picture him rising from his bed in the corner of a basement, the green ripples of the river flowing across the damp-stained ceiling. There is no light but the thin smoke of dawn, but what need has he of light? He dresses. He eats but doesn't taste the bitter coffee and chunks of yesterday's bread. His mother, for surely he is too young to have a wife, prepares a thin soup. He walks over the old brown snow to Charles Bridge. He takes off his cap his mother so lovingly placed on his head and puts it down where he put it down yesterday and the day before that…

I wrap myself in my unravelling skeins of narrative and

go and join you. It is only when I reach you at the other end of the bridge that I remember I haven't give him any money.

'I've found someone for you,' I say. The barge rounds a curve in the river and is gone. I drag you by the arm and show you the blind man. 'Look at that face.'

'Empty.'

'That's the whole point,' I argue.

'I can't take a picture of nothing.'

'Why not? I could write a novel about nothing.'

'That I can believe.'

We are still striking sparks off each other over coffee and pastries in a cafe at the end of the bridge. Your idea. On the walls bright wooden puppets rattle on strings like hanged men. Clowns, fiddle-players with red cheeks and orange hair, brown and white dogs with big red tongues leer at me. The coffee is too hot to taste.

I talk about the blind man. I know I am irritating you. Red blotches appear on both your cheeks. I know them well. 'But,' I persist, 'he must be cold and hungry and tired but no-one, and I mean no-one, gives him any money. I need to know why.'

You break off a piece of cake, lick each finger in turn. 'I'll tell you why.'

'Go on. Tell me.'

'He's boring.'

'Too glib. You can do better than that.'

'Okay. We all want something in return. Everybody hates short-changers. He is bad value for money. He's got "loser" written all over his face. Now that old guy with the squeeze-box. He's a star.'

I don't answer. Without asking whether you want any more coffee I take a third cup and drain the pot. You begin your ritual again using the two empty chairs at the table to spread out your equipment. Displacement activity. So you don't have to think that the conversation isn't about the blind man at all.

'Do you have to do that here?' I hiss through my teeth.

You don't look up. I'd rather you yell at me, strike me across the face, anything to tell me I exist.

'I'm going back to the bridge.'

Your head remains down. 'Okay.'

It is darker. Colder. The trinket sellers are packing up. The accordion player is now playing *La Vie en Rose*. The caffeine euphoria is gone. I am dispirited and dull as mud. The blind man is still there. His face is a face, his nose a nose, his eyes blank dead spaces. He is a blind man on a bridge. Prague is a tired old city under tired old snow. The surface of the river shines green like a fading bruise. One by one the lamps strung along the bridge snap on and glow like pearls. Does the blind man know that the sun has gone, the lamps lit? Can he feel the Vltava flowing eternally beneath his feet?

Suddenly the bridge is full of people, more than ever before, as if switched into being with the lights. Children. Families. They chatter like the starlings flying in to roost above them. The air crackles. A collective gasp catches the air. It rises and floats off across the green glass of the river. The floodlights of the Old City across the river burst like fireworks into the sky. The great pale castle hangs above the opposite bank; a heavenly host of angels spanning the black sky.

Madness grabs me. I run to the blind man. Pull his hand. Stroke his stone face. 'Can't you see?' I cry. 'This is beauty. You must see it! Look at it, damn you! Feel something for once in your life.'

He stares through my lunacy. He shouts something very loud and very long, which, of course, I can't understand. Except I can. His lips twist into cruel wires of anger. He spits and bubbling saliva freezes on my cheek. For a second the crowd about us jumps, looks, decides it is nothing, shrugs and moves on, pointing at the lights.

The blind man is a blind man. He stands as he always stands. I am a tourist, like all the other tourists. The crowd tosses glittering coins into the air. They spin and flash in the necklace of lights before falling into the biscuit tin of the accordion player.

And you are there at the end of the bridge. And I remember why you are always there at the end of the bridge. You are waiting for me. You will always wait for me to come back. You will wait until I am no longer blind.

PIG TALE

When the wife of the squire's pig-keeper gave birth to her twelfth and last child the handiwork of Satan was all too evident. The bristled pink baby girl had slipped squealing into this sinful world with a short, fat snout and nostrils like twin caverns.

Indeed, so much did the unfortunate creature resemble a pig, her father then fled the village in shame and his wife was drowned as a witch.

Thanks to the kindness of the villagers, who tossed her the occasional kitchen scrap, the child survived infancy. By the time she was five she had replaced her absent father as the squire's pig-keeper. She had a way with them, which wasn't surprising, the villagers said.

They called her Snout. She didn't expect favours and was not disappointed when she received curses and blows. After all, life was nasty, brutish and short for all mankind as well as pigs. She was no less happy than the villagers who spurned her and far more contented with her lot than the reclusive squire who had never been seen beyond his castle walls and whose wife was reputed to have a tongue like a rapier.

Understandably, Snout spent most of her time alone in the forest. From time to time a stranger would pass by; a soldier stained in blood, a peddler clanging iron pans or a hooded leper ringing his mournful bell. She never approached anyone, knowing that one glimpse of her would send men mad. The pigs, on the other hand, cared nothing for beauty. They were too clever. At night, she snuggled down between their soft flanks and was content.

And so her twelfth spring came. One morning, she lifted her head from her leaf-litter pillow and felt something was different. She could hear something.

At first, it was as faint as the stream that trickled nearby. It rustled with the breeze as sweet as summer rain, as mellow as rich butter, pure and piercing as a star in a velvet sky, as free as a skylark, softer than a lamb's first fleece. Louder it grew. Nearer it came, filling her head, rooting her to the ground. She was listening to music for the first time in her life.

Into the clearing limped a small band of women. They were dirty and bedraggled, their habits and wimples in rags. But they were singing. Snout could not believe such a heavenly sound could come from the mouths of people. All she had ever heard from such mouths before were curses and raucous laughter.

She ducked behind an oak tree. The women stopped by the ruins of an old manor house deserted many years before. Its tumble-down walls were toadstool-damp and smothered in ivy. But it boasted a roof of sorts and the skeletal remains of a tower from which a single rook cawed in greeting.

The chanting stopped. The women looked to each other and silently crossed themselves and Snout knew they had decided to make this place their home.

A routine was quickly established. The chanting began before dawn. Hidden in the trees, Snout listened in rapture. Then the women ate a breakfast as frugal as her own and then set about their tasks. They toiled all day, clearing, building, planting and sowing, without stopping, always praying or singing, until the sun slipped behind the tower. Only then did they stop and take another simple meal before retiring. When it rained they sheltered and stitched and wove, telling stories, and of course, singing.

How Snout ached to join them but she knew she would not be welcome even if she could summon the courage. But she watched and waited and once they slept, exhausted by their labours, she slipped away and tried to coax from her throat the sound that slipped with such ease from theirs. At first, all she could produce was a croak as rough as a hog's bristle, but slowly it softened to sweet honey, rich and pure. And when the women prayed, she prayed. And when they sang, she sang so that they thought the forest echoed their sounds with more sweetness than they themselves could manage. But she never approached them. She was in too much awe.

Until one morning, one of the sisters came across her when she had strayed from the others in search of succulent forest mushroom. When she saw Snout she shrieked and scattering her basket of mushrooms, ran back to the others claiming that she had seen the devil himself, his giant nostrils aflame, and his eyes blazing with evil. The ladies crossed themselves to ward off the evil that had come amongst them.

For the first time in her life Snout fell asleep sobbing with loneliness. Even the kind faces of her pigs could not console her. The next day she moved deeper into the forest where she could no longer hear the sound that pierced her heart.

She was away for many weeks during which the pigs rooted out all the goodness from the earth and became as empty in the bellies as Snout was of love and consolation. She cared nothing for her discomfort, but she could not let her beloved animals starve. She picked up her hazel switch and guided her pigs back towards the women.

The moment the newly mended tower emerged above the trees, she knew something was wrong. At first, with a thump of her heart, she thought the women had gone, so silent was their dwelling. But then she saw them huddled disconsolately by the gates like the fallen stones they worked so hard to clear. But there was no singing. The music had gone.

Terror seized her but curiosity made her bold. She hoisted the plumpest of the newest litter under her arm and advanced towards them.

The woman stared in horror as the dirt-streaked apparition of a human pig with its squealing child cradled in her arms emerged from the scrub. 'The sound. The beautiful sound,' she said. 'Where has it gone?'

The women were too stunned to run away. One thin voice struggled from the mouth of the oldest of the women who seemed to be in charge. She did not cry out when she saw Snout, although the mushroom-gathering girl had the decency to look ashamed. 'We have lost our voices,' the old woman croaked. 'Because of our sins.'

'Sins?' asked Snout.

'We fled our last convent because of the plague. We did not attend to the needs of our sick sisters. We ran like cowards and we were saved. We thought we were so clever. We sang in praise of our cleverness. And our singing was beautiful. We knew it. It puffed us up. But our music was nothing but selfishness and self-congratulation. God watched us as we built a temple to our pride and cowardice and now He has punished us. Now when we want to praise him, we have no voice.'

'I shall sing for you,' said Snout, with a simple dignity that would not disgrace the most high of ladies. The nuns could only watch with open mouths as the ugly pig-child began to sing. Even the litter-runt in her arms was stilled. As the sweet sound rose through the trees to the clear sky, the old woman lowered herself to the ground on creaking knees. 'Thank God. This is a miracle. St Anthony has sent his daughter to us.'

'Saint Anthony, Mother?' queried the youngest and least clever of the women.

'Do you not know your book of Saints, Sister Boniface?

The pig is sacred to Saint Anthony. He has come to save us.' And immediately she felt her singing voice return to her, deep and mellow. It joined that of Snout. One by one, the others took up the sweet melody, their faces glowing in joy and thankfulness.

And so, the years passed. The convent of Saint Anthony flourished. It became famous for its music, especially the wonderfully pure voice of Sister Antonia. Rumour had it that she was a great beauty, but modesty made her cover her face. She was well-liked by the people who lived scattered about the forest and in the village that lay nearby in the shadow of the squire's castle. She was a familiar sight in her grey robes, with her canvas bags of forest plants with which she tended the sick and prepared the dead for burial.

One day, Sister Antonia set out one sharp autumn morning when the leaves hung crisp and frost-tipped from the trees in order to lay out the body of the old squire who had departed this mortal earth the day before.

She was ushered into his chamber at the very top of the tallest tower by his widow who barked out strict orders that the leather mask which was still tied to his grey face was not to be removed. Antonia nodded meekly and the widow left her to her task.

Perhaps, the mask became detached by accident. God moves in a mysterious way. However it happened, before long, Antonia was face to face with the squire who was her father. A lesser mortal might have been stung with bitterness and hatred when she saw the familiar short, fat snout and cavernous nostrils but she merely smiled and continued her task.

MER DE GLACE

The lobby grew cluttered with trunks and unclaimed luggage. Rats were leaving France as if it were sinking. Each day more rooms were shut up and shrouded; each meal an ordeal of whispers among the polished glasses, the silver forks and starched white figured damask linen. Shadows crept to fill the empty spaces, silence muffled every corridor and staircase until two new gusts came down to breakfast one morning, the optimism of youth shining from their cheeks. A young man and a girl. Fair-haired and wholesome.

Laura leaned towards her husband who was reading an old copy of the *Morning Post*. 'They look friendly. Introduce us, please,' she asked Charles. He continued reading. She sipped her coffee.

She summoned the waiter in her faltering French. At this, the new young man smiled from across the room. She should have looked away – she was after all, and married women had to preserve their dignity and reputation – but she liked his grey eyes too much for that, even she was a married woman and, after all, and married women had to preserve their dignity and reputation. Only, the cloud of war that hung over them all was already rewriting the rules. She could feel the scratch of the moving pen on her skin.

The young man turned to the window and the misted rooftops. His companion chewed her plait amiably. He reached over the table and slapped her hand at which she giggled and slapped him back.

Laura stirred her coffee. 'I can't quite make them out. What do you think?'

Charles turned a page.

Beyond the windows another summer's day was easing itself to its full brilliance. The glaciers were retreating, the meadows were scorched, their flowers wilted, but still the river thundered on. During the sweet, sticky nights when sleep eluded her, its constant chunter shared her insomnia.

'Please, my dear. I'm trying to read a complex article about the Austro-Hungarians. I can't concentrate if you keep interrupting.'

Laura bit her lip. When she first met Charles she had fallen in love with his calm reason. Having been brought up as the baby of a house that was never silent, a house that resounded to the petty squabbles of five sisters, she had been flattered by his quiet attention. But she'd already forgotten how to speak to him and he no longer listened. What she had learned was how not to make a noise when she cried.

The waiter placed a boiled egg on the table. Charles folded his newspaper and picked up a spoon. 'Your eyes are very bright today, Laura. Doctor Parkin was right to suggest the Alps. The mountain air suits you.' In fact, Chamonix had been Laura's idea. The doctor had recommended Baden-Baden, but Charles had put his foot down. And she wondered how much mountain air she had breathed since she wasn't allowed to leave the hotel. She had lost her delight in books; her delight in life. What was there to do but spend her days in their room, staring at the carved and painted furniture?

'You'd think,' said Charles, 'that a hotel of this calibre would understand the concept of "lightly boiled". This is concrete.'

He pushed the plate away and picked up his newspaper. It was the first he had come across since they had arrived and he had pounced on it like a hawk on a rabbit. Laura poured more coffee from the pot and, inhaling its dark bitterness, resumed her observations. The girl was toying with the crumbs left on her plate and the man was watching her and jotting notes in his book.

‘I know who they are,’ she said. ‘Hansel and Gretel. He has worked out a plan so they won’t get lost in the forest. He will drop the crumbs behind them to make a trail. But it won’t work. The birds will eat the crumbs and the dark forest will close over them. They will never escape.’

Charles threw his newspaper across the table. ‘Can’t a man have some peace and quiet?’ His egg and spoon clattered to the floor. ‘I don’t know why I bother. This is such an old edition. We could already be at war.’

Hansel and Gretel rose from their table. When they’d gone, Laura whispered. ‘I think they’re German.’

‘Who?’

‘Hansel and Gretel. The couple by the window.’

Charles glanced about the empty room. ‘Are you sure you’re not feverish again? Besides, there won’t be any Germans here now. They’ll all be back home preparing for war. They knew what was up the moment the Archduke was assassinated.’

Laura laughed. Charles’s features sharpened. ‘I fail to see any humour in the situation. I sometimes think your misfortune has affected your mind.’

‘You are right. It isn’t funny. Nothing is funny anymore.’ She forced herself to her feet. ‘I’m tired. I’m going to lie down.’

Charles’s manner changed on the instant. ‘My dear. You should have said before. I apologise for my earlier outburst, but it is the fault of the Kaiser.’ He rapped the newspaper with his knuckles. ‘Impossible to believe he shares the same blood as our King. Let me take your arm.’

Laura had lied. She wasn’t weary, at least not in her body. That fizzed and spat like fat in a pan. As soon as Charles left her to return to his breakfast she flung open the shutters and leaned over the balcony. The town was going about its business. Carts thronged the streets. Neighbours hailed each other across the river. Below her the crashing of pots and the hot greasiness of lunch being prepared drifted up from the kitchens. A boy was sweeping the flags of the hotel terrace, dragging out tables and chairs, brushing fallen leaves from the canopied swing-seat. He was whistling between his teeth. Behind him, the river tumbled over heaps of smoothed boulders. The colour and texture of onyx, it rushed on, never changing, ever moving. How long would it take before the water she could see poured into the Rhone? And how long before it disgorged into the dazzling blue of the Mediterranean? When a fisherman dragged his nets ashore in Corsica, when his gasping, silver treasure slithered into the baskets he would later carry to market, would he see that same water? And if some of that same water glistening on one fish's back later splashed on the market floor, how long would it be before the sun reclaimed it, sucked it up, to fall as snow on the peaks that now shimmered through the mist? For the journey did not begin here. It started up there in the ice that had creaked and cracked high above her centuries before; ice that had felt the weight of mammoths.

So what then of the looming war? What did it mean to rivers, glaciers and mountains? And what then of the loss of one child, a child who had never breathed air nor drank water, compared with such enormity?

Threads of mist lay in loose skeins across the valley and shawled the white Massif, but as she watched, the threads unravelled and the peaks revealed themselves to her. They didn't roar or splash like the river; they didn't chatter and clatter like the servants in the kitchens but they spoke to her.

She only wished she knew what they were saying.

The effort exhausted her. The moment slipped from her

grasp. The mist closed in again. She shivered, closed the shutters and lay down on the bed.

She must have slept. Sunlight striped the wall and Charles was leaning over her. 'I'm sorry not have come up before, but I have met the most interesting fellow newly arrived from London. Morris – that's his name – says that if war comes, the British Army will soon trounce our enemies. He also says he can find me a suitable military posting so I won't miss the show. I suggested that he and I went for a stroll to mull things over. You don't mind, do you?'

She closed her eyes. 'Not at all.'

'Splendid. What glory awaits us all. Something to tell the children, eh?'

'What children would these be, Charles? Dr Parkin told me…'

'Doctors aren't always right, you know.'

'Shouldn't you go down? You don't want to keep Mr Morris waiting. She sat up. 'By the way. This war. It made you angry at breakfast. And now it's a glorious show. What's changed?' But he'd gone.

She ran out on the balcony in time to see him striding out swinging his Alpenstock, in animated conversation with a squat man with no neck. 'Onward Christian soldiers, marching as to war,' she muttered.

It was only when someone coughed that she realised she'd been heard. Below her Hansel's tanned face peered up at her. He was then joined by Gretel who waved her straw hat like a banner. 'My brother has ordered me to wear this to prevent…' She began in English but floundered.

'Freckles,' said Laura. The girl giggled.

'Eva and I are about to have lunch,' said the young man. 'Join us.'

'I can't.'

'Are you a prisoner?' said Eva.

'No, but I have...' She chose her words with care. 'I have been ill. I need to rest.'

'You can rest here,' said Eva.

'Indeed you can. It is most pleasant in the shade.'

After introductions had been made and hats compared, Laura found herself seated at a small table beneath a plane tree with a glass of wine before her and a cushion at her back. Hansel's real name was Theo Strauss. He was studying law, which he loathed.

'He wants to be a poet,' said Eva. 'He and Papa had a row about it, but Theo will have his way. He always does'

'Frau Thompson does not want to know that.'

'Laura, please. You make me sound old.'

'How old are you?'

'Eva!'

'I don't mind. I'm twenty-five.'

'Theo is twenty-three and I am sixteen.'

'Don't lie. You are fifteen and only just that.'

Eva pouted. 'You sound more like Papa every day.'

Theo explained that his father had asked him to take Eva on a European tour to complete her education.' But she refuses to learn anything. She is hopeless.'

Eva pulled a face. She began to strip lengths of straw from her hat and drop them to the ground. Theo grabbed it. 'I thought I told you to put your hat on your head, not your lap.'

'Poof!' Eva snatched it back, stood up, slapped it down on her seat and sat on it.

Laura was amused. 'You remind me so much of myself. I was the baby of a big family so I got everyone's cast-off. I once threw a pair of perfectly serviceable boots to our neighbour's pig.'

'What happened?'

'It gobbled them up.'

'I wish I'd thought of that.'

'Don't encourage her,' said Theo firmly although he was not angry. 'She already admires you too much.'

'I'm very ordinary.'

'Oh you are not ordinary at all,' exclaimed Eva, piling salad onto her plate. 'You are quite beautiful. Theo said your hair is like golden thistledown and that you are a princess locked in marriage to an evil wizard.'

'That is quite enough, Eva. And hold your fork properly. You are not a peasant.' Theo's anger silenced her and she said nothing more until the effects of the wine and food once more softened his eyes.

When the meal was over, Laura and Eva moved to the swing-seat. The shadows of the plane-trees crept inch by inch across the terrace. A soft breeze rolled down from the mountains, rustling the dry leaves above them. Chaffinches pecked for crumbs at their feet. Two doves were calling to each other and bees lumbered through the heavy afternoon air. The seat creaked as it swung, its fringe rippled and Eva snored gently, her arm thrown across Laura's lap. Theo remained at the table, reading. Absorbed and without self-regard, he melted into the scenery. Laura looked past him to the mountains, their whiteness merging with the pale sky behind a veil of shimmering light. She fanned herself with Eva's flattened hat. 'I feel like a Lotus Eater. Do you know Tennyson's poetry?'

Theo closed his book. 'Of course. "On the hills like Gods together, careless of mankind." Shall I order tea?'

'No thank you. I am sipping nectar.'

He smiled. 'Tea, Eva?'

His sister moved her arm but did not wake. 'She is fortunate to have you to care for her,' said Laura.

‘She doesn’t think so.’

‘Where will you go when you leave France?’

‘We had planned to tour England. But that is now out of the question.’

‘The war,’ she said watching a line of schoolboys march past.

‘Yes.’

‘If war comes…’

‘It will come.’

‘Will you fight?’ She had a sudden image of Charles and Theo rushing towards each other, sabres aloft.

‘I have asthma,’ he said. ‘Eva does not know yet but as soon as war is declared I shall take her to Zurich. Our family is to gather there. And you? What plans have you made?’

She shook her head. She couldn’t think ahead nor imagine anything other than leaning back, suspended in the air, beneath the glittering mountains. She wanted to catch the butterfly moment in her hand and hold it captive, feel it fluttering until she chose to let it go. The purring of the doves, the flop of a leaf onto a table, Eva’s crumpled hat, the rush of the river behind her, a hawk hanging above the valley, the sun on its slow decline, the scent of rain in the next valley.

‘When I first came here,’ she said. ‘The mountains seemed too large. I was terrified they would crash down on me.’

‘And now?’ asked Theo batting a fly from his face.

‘Like they want to embrace me and keep me safe. Like a mother folds herself over her child.’ A sob caught her by surprise. Theo leaned forward in his chair, not questioning but giving her space to speak further and before she was aware she was doing it, before she had time to regret her indiscretion, she was telling him about the miscarriage and the doctor’s fear that she would never have another child.

‘I detect your loss has left a shard of ice in your heart,’ he said.

Had it?

Mountain weather is volatile and clouds were now rolling through the valley. Thunder growled. Wind rattled the trees and lifted the leaves from the ground. The birds had stopped chirping but the river tumbled down to the Rhone, to the sea, to the sky to fall as rain, to trickle, splash, rush, pour and tumble again and again and again. And here she was.

‘Laura!’

And there was Charles. He took her arm and with a cold nod to Theo, pulled her from the seat and propelled her into the hotel, up the stairs and into their room. ‘Have you taken leave of your senses? Here we are on the very precipice of war and I find you intimate with Germans.’

Laura gripped the bedstead. ‘At breakfast you said there were no Germans here. Don’t you remember? All Germans are at home preparing for war.’

Charles raised his hand. ‘Morris says there may well be spies working here.’

An explosion of mirthless laughter ripped through her. Charles shook his head. ‘You are such an innocent, my dear. By the way, I have asked him to join us for dinner. I want you downstairs by eight. And wear your pearls.’

Laura couldn’t move. Her limbs were lead weights. A ball of ice was swelling within her. She felt both very small and as mighty and implacable as the mountains over whose heads, inky rags of cloud were now pouring. If she chose to she could rip the paper from the walls, claw the paint from the wardrobe, shatter the windows and leap to the ground and run through the streets, a screaming harpy. Instead, she had to pull each frozen word from her mouth. ‘No Charles. I will not wear your pearls and I will not come down for dinner.’

‘If that is your decision, I will respect it. Morris will understand. I have already informed him of your misfortune.’

‘Our misfortune.’

‘Indeed, Laura. Our misfortune.’ He patted her arm. She shook the gesture off and he left her.

She shrank to think that Charles could freely dispense private information that had taken a pair of soft, grey eyes to extract from her. ‘My wife is a semi-invalid, you know, since she lost our first child. That’s why I brought her here despite the imminence of war. Physically she is recovering but I am somewhat concerned about her mental state.’

Damn him! She slammed the window against the rain that was now sheeting across the town. The terrace was water-logged; the swing-seat rocked like a ship at sea. Rain lashed the flagstones and the wind’s teeth shredded the sodden ribbons of Eva’s hat that lay abandoned on the seat.

The rain fell all night and on and off for the next three days as July became August. Bloated clouds filled the valley, blotting out the crags and peaks. The river rose and spilled into cellars and kitchens, but Laura, curled up in her bed, knew nothing of this only that she was living up to Charles’s stereotype of a weak and silly woman. She hated herself for it, but couldn’t see how to stop until one afternoon – she didn’t know what day of the week it was – Eva knocked and entered. She flumped down at the foot of the bed, chewing her plait.

‘Are you very ill?’

‘Not at all.’

‘Theo and I miss you terribly. We have been worried.’

‘There was no need.’ She felt ashamed of their concern but at the same time she tingled in its glow. Suddenly, bored with the role she had imposed upon herself, she finally became aware of how others might see her. She touched her hair. It was thick and matted. Her nightdress clung to her, grey and crumpled. Medicine bottles cluttered the mantelpiece and discarded clothes were strewn across the floor.

'Theo says you have an illness of the heart.'

'Did he? Then he is wrong. There is nothing wrong with my heart. It's more simple than that. My husband says I must not speak to Germans.'

'I see.' Eva opened the shutters. The clouds had gone; the sky was a sheet of blue. The mountains remained.

'Theo thought as much,' she said. 'Tell me. If your husband knew I was here, would he kill us?'

'Charles?' The very idea of her husband, of all people, bursting into the room armed with a gun, sword or even his Alpenstock was so ridiculous that she giggled. Eva joined in and the more they did so the more ridiculous her prolonged sulk was. 'Run downstairs,' she said when she had regained control. 'Tell Theo I shall be on the terrace in fifteen minutes.'

It wasn't difficult. She didn't have to lie. Charles was so regular in his habits that she knew he and Morris wouldn't return to the hotel until four-thirty by which time she was calmly seated alone on the terrace, reading a novel. And if her cheeks were more flushed than usual, and even if Charles noticed, she could put it down to the alpine air.

She, Eva and Theo soon established a routine. Lunch on the terrace, tea on the swing seat followed. Their conversation was mainly about music and literature. Laura was ashamed that, despite Theo's low opinion of Eva's learning, she knew far more about them than she did. Theo recommended books for her and she read thirstily. Her French improved and she asked Theo to teach her German. She was no linguist but when they were apart, how she longed for the joy of sitting next to him with a pile of books between them, watching the changing emotions in his eyes as she stumbled over his language, sensing his closeness, stealing herself for his warm breath on her cheek, the brush of his hand against hers.

The only thing she dared not do was leave the hotel. Petty acts of defiance were easy enough; blatant disobedience was quite another matter. But when Eva mentioned that she and Theo were planning to walk up to the famous Mer de Glace the following day, she knew she had to be there with them.

'We shall walk,' said Eva. 'But there is a new railway to the glacier. You could manage that, couldn't you?'

'I don't know. I will have to ask my husband.'

'Poof. I will never marry if I have to ask permission to do what pleases me.'

'That is enough, Eva' said Theo. 'You know nothing.'

'And you're horrid.'

She stomped over to the river. 'She is disappointed,' he said watching his sister hurl pebble after pebble into the river. 'She never knew our mother. I wish you could come on your own.'

'Is it for Eva that you ask or for yourself?'

'Laura,' he said, 'false naivety is not becoming.'

Charles was pleasingly relaxed over dinner. Laura suspected that he and Morris had shared more than animated conversation and had themselves decided to see this famous 'meteorological phenomenon'. The excursion by train to the glacier was easily decided on. He had patted her arm and said how relieved he was that she was almost back to her old self. Only Morris, too, was to be included.

The carriages soon filled. Laura hadn't been aware that so many tourists still remained in the town. She had assumed that there carriage would be half empty but she found herself glumly wedged between Charles and a Belgian woman who, clearly expecting a famine, was distributing lumps of bacon and bread amongst her offspring.

The little engine nosed the carriages up the winding track. One moment she had a fleeting view of the valley and the next the train plunged her into dank blue forest and dripping tunnels before once more bursting out into the light. The air grew increasingly chillier and she felt thin and stretched, distant from reality.

And yet, even here, the talk was of war. The word scuttled up and down the carriage like a rat. Morris had no other topic of conversation. In order to catch what he was saying over the snorts of the engine and the rattle of the carriage, Charles had to lean away from her across the aisle to where Morris perched, his Alpenstock gripped between his tweed knees.

The train lurched ever upwards. Women crossed themselves, silent lips moving; children screamed and gasped as the incline steepened or the track seemed to cling to the very edge of a precipice. Morris had finally run out of war platitudes and was reading aloud from his guidebook. 'The *Mer de Glace*, or rather, Sea of Glass.' He nodded to Charles. '—Although River would be the more appropriate word, but that's the French for you – is more than eleven kilometres (what on earth is that in miles?) in length and moves at a speed of…'

Laura turned away. The train slowed to negotiate a viaduct before levelling out alongside the Montenvers Hotel. Its terrace was already dotted with fashionable hats, their brims competing with the table parasols. The engine chugged into the station and wheezed to a halt. Its passengers stumbled out onto the platform, huddling into their coats and blowing on their hands, exclaiming at the sharpness of the thin, icy air, hovering, uncertain what to do.

Charles took her arm and led her to the viewing platform overhanging the glacier. Morris scurried off, pushing past others to secure the services of a guide who, with his ladder and thick socks for hire, was shouting his prices.

'I think it would be best if you wait here,' Charles said banging his hands together, his breath clouding around his face. 'Retire to the ladies' waiting-room if you get too cold. We will meet you at the hotel for lunch. Shall we say in half an hour?'

Morris bowed and he and Charles made their way down the steps cut into the rock.

Laura felt light-headed, like a kite tugging on its string. Perhaps it was the altitude. It wasn't the sight of the glacier. She had expected a field of diamonds but it was a dirty blanket of icy grit. Tourists were moving aimlessly on its surface. With their ladders and lengths of rope, the scene resembled a game of snakes and ladders spread out below her. Behind her, the train driver and his companions were passing round a bottle of beer and exchanging desultory remarks and short grunts of laughter as they stoked, watered and polished the engine. Wafts of sulphurous smoke drifted down and melted in the milky blue of the mountains that guarded the head of the glacier. She checked Morris's guidebook he had left behind. They were called 'Les Grandes Jorasses'. She didn't know what the name meant but it sounded suitably lofty.

'You came, then?' Theo sat down beside her. He slipped his haversack off his back.

'Did you doubt me?'

He considered her remark. 'No, but I…'

'Charles is playing snakes and ladders with Morris.'

'I see,' he said but clearly didn't.

'What does "Grandes Jorasses" mean?'

'I don't know.' He was out of breath and distracted. 'Does it matter?' Why was he so brittle? Had the altitude frozen his friendliness?

'I suppose not.'

They both pretended to admire the view; she looked left; he right.

'Where's Eva?'

He pointed to where she was crouched on the snow, plait in her mouth and a pencil and sketchbook in her hand.

'Laura,' he began. Then stopped. He reached out his hand. Instantly she was elated and deflated by the banality of his gesture. Was this what she had come here for? She didn't know but their hands didn't touch. Instead, a babble of voices broke out around them. One of the railway workers had left his fellows and was pushing his way towards the hotel. Another began to slide and slither down the steps towards the glacier, shouting and gesticulating. Soon the whole mountainside was stirred up as if an ant's nest had been poked by a giant stick.

'What is it? What's happening?' Theo was now on his feet, struggling with his haversack, calling to Eva.

Charles returned. She held her breath, bracing herself for his anger but he merely bowed to Theo. 'It would seem that your country has declared war on France. It will not be long before our countries are enemies.' He held out his hand.

'Indeed so.' Theo took the hand but looked stiff and uncomfortable. He then turned to Laura and bowed. 'Goodbye, Mrs Thompson. My sister and I must leave for Switzerland immediately.' Helping Eva to her feet, he guided her steps over the ice towards the track that led back down to the valley.

She took a step forward. 'Wait!' she cried stupidly without knowing why. Her voice rang around the rocks, before fading away. Eva turned her head briefly but Theo didn't hesitate or turn round.

'It's time we went home,' said Charles softly. He paused before whispering, 'You are so, so lovely. I had not seen it until now.'

The platform was already crowded with ashen, silent faces peering at the sky in the expectation of thunderbolts crashing down from the blue or at least something more significant than a little toy engine with its comical funnel and scarlet carriages.

And then she noticed something else. 'Where's Morris?'

'We had a small difference of opinion down on the glacier. When he heard the news, he said that if he had a pistol, he would have shot every German in sight without compunction. Man, woman or child.'

'And what did you say to that?'

'That he was a pompous ass.'

They both smiled. He took her hand and folded it in his. Theo and Eva were out of sight and she would only retain scraps of them in years to come. She knew they would prosper. Like raindrops on the ocean, nothing left a mark on people like Theo. But what of Charles? And the moment she posed the question, the mountains and the ice melted away, and she saw him in a ditch, splattered with blood-streaked mud, his eyes wide and staring, seeing nothing. She clutched her fur collar and stumbled.

'Are you all right?' he said and she was. And so was he. The mountains glittering in the brittle sunlight could teach her nothing. 'Let us not take the train back,' she said, tugging his sleeve. 'Let's walk.'

The snow kicked up by their boots circled them in luminescence until they entered the shadow of the pines leaving the sea of glass to itself.

HEALTH AND SAFETY

There she goes, lighting up again. She takes a drag, checks the tip to see it's lit, then goes back to staring into space. It's not long before smoking will be banned in public places. It's in all the papers. Cerise says that if everyone gives up the evil weed, Health and Safety will only go and find something else that's bad for us.

'Everything that's fun is,' she says and laughs. 'Bubble gum next,' and she blows a great big pink balloon that explodes with a smack against her cheek. She's forty-five. Same age as me but everybody assumes she's younger.

When I got this job, well before Cerise arrived, there was an urn for boiling water and drums of powdered tea and coffee. It was the Station Buffet then with thick white cups and saucers and plates of sandwiches under a glass dome like the one in *Brief Encounter*. Ham, egg and cress, cheese and pickle, all of them curling at the edges by midday. It's the Green Oasis now with plastic palms and camels trekking across the walls, although what it's got to do with railways is beyond me.

'Camel trains,' Cerise explains. 'Bringing a bit of the exotic into our humdrum existence.' But, like most of what she goes on about, doesn't make sense.

We now sell four varieties of tea and twenty coffees but it's still not what I would call a café. My dream is to have a small place of my own with lace curtains and tablecloths, bone china and tea-cosies. I'd sell scones and home-made jam and there'd be little posies of flowers on every table instead of tin ashtrays like here. Sheba would be curled up in her basket next to the till.

'Health and Safety wouldn't allow that,' Cerise said when I told her about it one quiet day.

Health and Safety? Don't make me laugh. What do they

know? There's no such thing. Life is neither healthy nor safe for any living thing whatever these busybodies say. When the RSPCA found Sheba locked in a shed, she was in a right state. You could see her ribs and someone had taken a blunt knife to her tail. You wouldn't think she was the same dog now. She loves her food and I give her all the leftovers from here. She's got a bit of a tummy on her and the vet told me off but I told her straight. 'If you'd seen her when I first did you would be delighted.' Anyway, she's not fat. She's cuddly. Sheba that is, not the vet. It's all a matter of balance. One size doesn't fit all.

Sheba's favourite nosh used to be the steak and kidney pies I brought home from The Feathers before I got the sack. Can't blame Grumpy Jack, really. He said he was running a fucking pub not a fucking drop-in centre for the fucking social services and that allowing ne'er do-wells credit and letting them slob about all day stinking the place out and feeding their mangy dogs was not what I was paid for. But you can do both, can't you? Serve the paying public for decent service and looking after the desperate? People need to know someone cares about them. Not some Jobsworth spouting rules. Not Health and Safety either.

Any road, I'm here now and Sheba's got used to the sweet stuff. I don't think dogs have memories. You'd never think Sheba had ever been abused. She's so trusting. She runs up to everyone for a kiss and a cuddle and gets one too. But one day she might not. I mean, people can be funny about dogs, can't they? But I can't forget the past. Even with sleeping-pills. Some things, once seen, are never forgotten.

That's why I'm twitching like a nervous frog about her with the cigarettes over by the window. And the fact she's been nursing that latte decaff for two hours now. It wasn't even hot when I poured it. I think there's something wrong with the machine. I called maintenance four times last week but no-one's turned up yet. I apologize to customers all the time. Cerise took me to one side the other day and told me not to. 'Never trouble trouble till trouble troubles you,' she said.

'That's the trouble,' I said. She laughed. But I wasn't joking.

She wasn't here when it happened. She has no idea.

The girl with the fags and the cold coffee is a pretty little thing or would be if she smiled. As well as the smoke that's hanging around her there's something else too. I don't know what you call it. The smell of bad choices and missed opportunities that greets you when you go home to an empty flat. I'd be the same if I didn't have Sheba.

She glances at her watch and then the clock behind the counter. 'It's always five minutes fast,' I call over but she doesn't seem to hear me. Then she looks at the door before taking another long suck on her ciggie as if she's drawing life itself from it.

There she goes again, screwing the butt down on top of the others and lighting another. She must have money to burn although she doesn't look rich. She doesn't look anything, really. She's young enough to be my daughter. Hark at me. I've not got a daughter. At least, not since Patricia walked out and never came back. No wonder I worry. She could be sleeping in a cardboard box somewhere for all I know. God, I hope not. No. Mustn't think about it. Plenty of other people to worry about. Pat told me before she left I was an interfering old witch.

The station loudspeaker in the corner crackles into life. It does so every five minutes during the day and I don't even notice it but at this time of night it makes my heart race.

She doesn't move a muscle. In a world of her own.

The ten-thirty to Derby's rolling in now. Platform two instead of four because it's ten minutes late. The two men in old anoraks who've been checking the racing pages at the table nearest to the till dash off like hounds out of the starting gates. 'Cry Havoc and let slip the dogs of war,' I call after them. Cerise laughs at me when I come out with stuff like that. 'You're weird, you are,' she says. But it's not me that's odd. It's her. Her son's in prison and her daughter is eighteen and already has two kids and now lives with a drug-dealer. And all she does is shrug her shoulders and say, 'What can you do?' And laugh.

A whistle blows on the far side of the station. An engine judders, belches a lungful of diesel smoke and slides out of the station on a slick of black oil. Now there's only the stopping service to Peterborough to come and the ten fifty to Birmingham New Street and then I can close up.

I'm stocking up the fridge with bottles of fizzy water ready for tomorrow when the Peterborough train rolls in. The remaining few coffee-drinkers get up. Now there's just me and her. I clear their tables and get out the mop and fill a bucket. I count the pastries. Still four Apple Danishes and a Cinnamon Swirl left for Sheba. One young man with rings hanging off one ear nearly chose that but I told him it had been sitting there since yesterday so he bought a Kit-Kat instead.

I'm supposed to fill in a form listing all the perishable stuff that has to be thrown away at the end of the day but I don't bother.

Mrs Aspinall, who comes in her little black suit from head office to audit the paperwork every six months, is a suspicious so-and-so.

'Sell every last item, every single day, do we?' she said once all sarky-like but she leaves me alone now. She must have heard about what happened. Like I had something to do with it and it's contagious or something.

The old station master had to take early retirement. Nerves shot to pieces, they said. But he didn't see anything. He was fast asleep in his cubby-hole until all hell broke loose. Then he went out into the car park and threw up over a shiny white Mercedes.

I had to make a statement and go to the Coroner's Court. I told them how the man sat for hours in here, just like this girl, then walked out as calm as you like. Then stepped off in front of the non-stop to New Street. There was a helluva screech of brakes but it was far too late, of course.

I told them what I'd seen. They never asked me for details else so I didn't tell them more than the obvious.

He'd been getting on my nerves, see? He sat there for hours with one flipping mean espresso, chain-smoking and flicking ash all over the table I'd just wiped. Well, I'd been sacked once before for being kind so I also said, 'There's an ashtray, you know. How about using it?' He looked through me as if I wasn't there or wasn't important enough for him to waste his eyesight on so I went on, 'Grown roots, have you?' When he still ignored me I did a Grumpy Jack and reminded him that the café was for paying customers only and that he'd better move to the waiting-room on platform one if he wasn't going to buy anything. Still ignored me.

The next time I went over with my cloth, he looked at as if he was seeing me for the first time and asked me if I had a moment to sit down. He wanted to ask my opinion about something important.

I told him I was too busy and went back to the counter. I was keeping my eyes on the pastries, see? I remember I counted them and smiled. Like tonight, there were exactly four Apple Danishes and a Cinnamon Swirl. Funny that. Maybe that's why I'm so on edge tonight. That man stubbed out his last cigarette and stood up. 'Thank you so much for your time,' he said quietly, closed the door carefully behind him, crossed the platform and jumped.

So that's why, when this girl starts filling up the ashtray quicker than the condensation is dripping puddles on the floor, I'm a bit, well. You know.

I move the chairs so I can mop by her table. 'I'm closing up as soon as the ten fifty's gone,' I say. It sounds awkward. Bossy even. I'm no longer any good at small-talk now. Besides, it's wasted on a dog.

'Thank you,' she says although I can't tell if she means it.

'Catching it, are you?' I don't mention she's already missed three Birmingham trains whilst she's been sat there smoking for England.

'Yes,' she says quickly.

Too quickly. I'm feeling peculiar. Light-headed. I step back. Only go and knock the bucket over, don't I? And while I'm all of a fluster, the loudspeaker makes me jump, echoing off the walls and making the bottles in the fridges rattle. The Birmingham train. The ten fifty.

Can't think. Stand there like a flaming lemon. Think of something. Dash behind the counter, grab the four Apple Danishes and the Cinnamon Swirl and push them in a bag so hard it splits. I catch her just as she gets to the door. Stand with my back flat against it. Icy air whistles through the gap. And I'm babbling like Cerise does into that mobile phone of hers. 'Here. Take them,' I say, shoving the greasy bag in her face. 'It's long way to Birmingham and there's no trolley-service on that train. They're really nice. Still fresh. They'll only go to waste. Health and Safety, you understand. We're not allowed to sell them the next day.'

She looks at me. Nothing. Blank as an empty ashtray. Then something happens and that grey dead look falls from her face. She smiles. The train clanks in, slows and the doors stutter open.

‘Thank you,’ she says quietly and touches me on the shoulder. Like a butterfly, it’s there and then it’s gone. She hurries across the platform and boards the train. She moves down the carriage and I can’t see her any more.

The wind bowls an empty Coke can along the platform and under a bench where it rocks to and fro, a loveless child. The train waits, its engine thrumming like a giant’s heart. Above it, I can hear the guard yell something to Barry who’s supposed to clean the toilets. Something about whether City stand a chance against Chelsea on Saturday. ‘Not a fucking chance, mate,’ grunts Barry and shuffles off to get his coat.

One shrill blast of the whistle. The doors close and the train moves off and that’s it for another day.

I go back in, right the bucket and mop up the mess. A thin trail of smoke still rises from the ashtray. I leave it there, set the alarm and lock up. I should clear it away – Healthy and Safety – but it’ll burn itself out and I know it will help me sleep to think of it sitting there, proof she was here in my café and she smiled at me and now she’s safely on her way to Birmingham. I caught a fleeting glimpse inside the carriage. All its lights were on. Had she thought of jumping? I dunno but there’s nothing for Sheba now. Never mind. I’ll buy her some chips on the way home. She’ll be pleased whatever I give her. That’s the thing about dogs. They take what comes and get on with it.

STILL LIFE WITH CUCKOO AND BULLDOZER

Follow the cuckoo. Follow the cuckoo as it flits from the hedge at the bottom of Penny's garden. Follow it to the ash-tree where it begins to call. Cuckoo. Cuckoo. Cuckoo. The sound hiccoughs through the brittle chill of the June morning. Soon the air will grow limp and flow with heat. Penny wakes in her room that overlooks the ash-tree. She goes to her window and watches a pale sun rise above liquid trees. Mist trails across the field beyond the garden. The field is empty. The cows that once swished lazy tails through clouds of flies have gone. The field has been sold for development. The sun rises for the last time over the long, cool grass, flecked with vetch and clover. The bulldozer is on its way.

Penny's mother passes her door on the way to the bathroom. 'Bloody bird. If I had a gun.' Penny's mother is thirty-nine and dreading her next birthday. Penny is sixteen and ripe for love.

Follow the cuckoo along the boundary of Fieldview Crescent to the fence-post at the bottom of Teresa's garden. Cuckoo. Cuckoo. Teresa turns over as far as her nine month foetus will let her and lies staring at the corner of the ceiling. Geoff snores beside her. The cuckoo is her enemy. It has been calling all day, every day for weeks. Why won't this baby be born? Will she never be rid of this parasite? It is drinking her blood. Eating her flesh. Growing fatter as she grows thin. The nursery is ready. The cot is ready. The drawers are full of nappies and babygros. Teresa is full of despair. The sun bursts through the mist and onto her face. Another hot day. Cuckoo. Cuckoo. Cuckoo.

The bulldozer is on its way. It is on a low-loader trundling down the bypass. Early commuters fume and tune their radios to find an alternative route. Or swear. Or run their fingers between their wet collars and their sore necks and overtake on blind bends. Harry narrowly misses death as a car hurtles towards him on the wrong side of the road. But this isn't his story. So we can skip the bit about him finding a lump in his groin that morning in the shower and get back to Fieldview Crescent.

Cuckoo. Cuckoo. The cuckoo is hiding in the holly bush in Sadie's garden. This prickly defender is the single unwelcoming feature of Sadie's property. There are two loungers and a drinks trolley on the patio. Beyond the double-glazed patio doors, through the lounge with its pink shag-pile, into the bedroom where china dolls in pantaloons and velvet bonnets pout from every available surface, is a double bed. Sadie doesn't hear the cuckoo. She drank half a bottle of gin last night. She was not alone then. But her visitor had to get home to his wife. So she is alone now in her short nylon nightie. Her fluffy slippers wait at the foot of the candlewick like patient pink bunnies.

Follow Penny on her way to school, which is on the far side of the old cowfield. She used to hop over the hedge and walk past the gentle beasts, but they are gone and the field is fenced off, so she has to walk around its edge. Cuckoo. Cuckoo. Where is that wandering voice? Penny did Wordsworth last term. The morning breeze lifts crisp grass sap into her nose. She breathes in its lingering dampness. Soon to evaporate. Soon to suffocate under bricks and concrete. She waves to Teresa, who is at her window. Teresa does not wave back. Geoff is laboriously grumbling through a bowl of cornflakes. Teresa stopped frying bacon when the morning sickness began. He hopes normal service will return when the baby comes. That will put the colour back in her cheeks. She won't have time to moon about then.

Sadie turns over. Her arm dangles over the edge of the bed like a flipper. Follow her dream where she is floating in a bright blue swimming-pool where the sun makes bright lozenges of light around her face. The water caresses her sagging cheeks. Soothes and calms. Peace at last.

Teresa was going to wash some windows. The sun shows up every mark. But that means going outside. She can't go outside. It is too hot. And the cuckoo is there, watching her with its bright, black eye. Cuckoo. Cuckoo. And when it stops for a second, there are the wood-pigeons burbling on the chimney-pot. She checks that the piece of hardboard she got Geoff to hammer across the fireplace is secure. The nails have worked loose but she can't go into the garage to fetch the hammer. That would mean opening the door. She sinks down on the hearth rug, defeated. The cuckoo begins again. She hates the baby.

Penny is sitting at the front of the class alternately writing carefully in her loopy script and sucking the end of her pen as Miss Hargreaves burbles about the foreign policy of Elizabeth I. She sounds like the wood pigeons on Teresa's chimney-pot. Penny can still hear the cuckoo. It is in the copse at the back of the tennis-courts. She and Willa have a semi-final to play at lunch-time. Willa has hay-fever, but Penny knows she will win, anyway.

The low-loader has stopped at the gate to the old cowfield. The compressed traffic, now released, whoops past with triumphant full-throttles. Two men jump down. Their chests are mahogany brown. They glisten with sweat. The bulldozer is unloaded. The low-loader and one man leave. The other man wipes his hand across his brow. His hair is bleached to a pale-gold by the sun. He stands in the dazzle of the sun. He is golden Apollo. Penny and Willa watch with open mouths, their racquets limp in their hands. The game is abandoned.

Penny's mother is pegging out the washing. She sees the bulldozer trundle up and down the field, gouging up the grass, hurling gouts of rust-coloured soil into the simmering air like a juggler. Fine particles drift over the hedge and settle on Penny's school shirts. Time for some coffee. She'll have it inside. That bloody bird is still at it. It had been her husband's idea to move to the country – 'For the peace and quiet.' Well, he's got that all right. The bloody crematorium's quiet as the grave. Never mind where his widow's fetched up. Stuck here with a bloody cuckoo and now a bulldozer. Trust him to dump her somewhere like Fieldview Crescent with its Legoland bungalows and rustic pergolas. She sees Teresa at her window. She waves and brightly mimes the action of drinking a cup of coffee. Teresa shakes her head. Suit yourself. Grumpy cow. Anyone would think no-one else ever got themselves up the spout. Her windows could do with a wash. She ought to do it now. There won't be time when she's had that baby.

Sadie finishes painting her nails and stretches out on top of the duvet until they dry. The telephone rings. She doesn't answer it. Can't spoil her manicure. If it's important, they'll ring back. She hears the cuckoo and the bulldozer, but they don't impinge on her consciousness. She is going to have her hair permed this morning.

Willa has gone. Her eyes water too much to stay outside. Penny lingers by the edge of the old cowfield that is now a lunar landscape. The drift of diesel oil wraps about her neck, pulling her onwards. The ground shakes and throbs beneath her feet although the bulldozer is at the far end of the field. It turns and comes towards her. She stands in the middle of the field like the lone student against the tank in Tieneman Square. The bulldozer stops a foot in front of her. It overpowers her. It blocks the sky. Close to, it is ugly, paint scraped, thickly encrusted with black grease. Its bucket snarls a shark's jaw greeting. She is bold, yet trembles. Powerful but submissive. The pit of her stomach melts like chocolate left too long in her hand. The engine falters. The silence is delicious and soft like warm pillows on her ears. The driver jumps down and clicks his teeth. Cuckoo. Cuckoo. Cuckoo.

Follow Teresa to the hall where the morning newspaper lies. She bends down slowly and picks it up and takes it back into the kitchen. She tears it up into long strips which she stuffs in the cracks around the windows. Sweat trickles into her eyes. She can still hear the cuckoo through the muffled roar of the bulldozer. The giant yellow monster is coming to gobble her up. She can cope with that. If only the cuckoo would leave her alone. Cuckoo. Cuckoo. Cuckoo.

Sadie puts her glass down on the drinks trolley and checks her watch. Half-past one. She stretches out on her front and undoes the hook on her bikini top. One hour to toast her back. Then roll over. The cuckoo has returned to the ash tree in Penny's garden. Soon it will move to the fence-post at the bottom of Teresa's garden. Round and round. Cuckoo. Cuckoo. Sadie doesn't hear it. One page of Danielle Steele; one glass of Waitrose white Lambrusco and she sleeps.

Penny watches him throw back his head and lift a bottle to his mouth. He drinks and drinks until the bottle is empty, warm foam trickling down the dirt-grained furrows of his chin. 'Catch!' He grins and tosses it in the air. It rises in a curve of kingfisher green brilliance and falls to the ground. 'Butterfingers.' Penny blushes and runs to it. She picks it up, trying to keep her eyes from the neck where the man's lips have sucked.

'You shouldn't drop litter,' she squeaks. She did so want her voice to sound deep brown.

'Is that right?' he says. His teeth are ice-white against

his brown face. He lights a cigarette. 'Want a drag?' Penny shakes her head quickly, then wishes she'd said yes. There is a silence. The cuckoo is in the hedge behind the hockey field. Cuckoo. Cuckoo.

Penny's Mum has had enough. She telephones her friend. 'There's a bloody cuckoo driving me mad. Fancy meeting me in town?' She puts on her white shoes that pinch and heads for the bus-stop. Follow the clack of her heels on the pavement. Brittle dry dust rattles around her bare legs. The sun flattens her head. She should have worn her white straw hat. The cuckoo cannot be heard above the traffic on the main road. She will buy herself another pair of shoes to celebrate. She has fifty-two pairs of shoes. They are all elegant. They all pinch.

Teresa is talking to the cuckoo. It has grown to the size of a dog and is sitting on the rosebush by the lounge window. 'What do you want?' she says. 'Cuckoo. Cuckoo,' says the cuckoo. The telephone rings. She answers it. Eventually. It is Geoff.

'Anything happening?'

'The cuckoo,' says Teresa slowly.

'Now remember. As soon as things start to happen phone the ambulance. Then phone me. I'm in a meeting but Sue will drag me out. You've got the number. I'm in Nottingham today, remember, not Leicester.'

'Yes.'

'Are you all right, love?'

'Fine.' She puts the phone down. Her back drags. She goes back to talk to the cuckoo. A hot flush of liquid cascades down her legs. She doesn't feel it. Cuckoos lay their eggs in other birds' nests. They are bigger than their victims. The cuckoo is as big as a horse. It has laid its egg in her belly.

'So, what's a pretty girl like you doing still at school?'

‘I’m doing my GCSEs then I want to do A levels.’

‘Is that right? I didn’t know I was talking to an intellectual.’

Penny blushes. ‘Do you think,’ she squeaks. ‘I might have a cigarette?’

His face is next to hers as he lights a cigarette from his. So close, she can taste his sweat. She is dizzy. She takes a large intake of smoke and staggers, her throat burning, her head ringing. The driver laughs. The bell goes. ‘I’ve got double maths now,’ Penny wheezes, her head hotly reeling.

‘What time does school finish?’

‘Quarter to four.’

‘I expect I’ll see you then. You can teach me some maths. Clever girl like you.’ He smiles and her body purrs.

She doesn’t hear the afternoon lesson. She sees white teeth and a bronzed torso. Him and her. Sharing cigarettes, stealing kisses. The cuckoo is in the tree that overhangs the bicycle sheds. Willa is jealous. Penny can’t wait until a quarter to four. She will borrow one of Willa’s lipsticks. She can’t decide between Hot Pink or Passion.

‘Pay attention, Penny.’

‘Sorry.’ Cuckoo. Cuckoo.

Sadie yawns and stretches. She sits up, holding her bikini top to her. The bulldozer driver is grinning at her over the hedge. He looks hot. Sadie waves the bottle of wine in the air over the noise of the throbbing idle of the powerful machine. The engine cuts out. The man is beside her. ‘Anything stronger?’

Sadie fastens her bikini slowly. ‘Plenty stronger,’ she smiles, pleased that her hair has turned out so well.

Teresa crouches on the lounge floor, her knees pulled up to her belly. She whimpers to the cuckoo. ‘Take your baby. Take it. I don’t want it.’ Her head twists from side to side. Her fingers tear up tufts of carpet.

The cuckoo is back on the ash tree at the bottom of Penny's garden. The bulldozer is still. Its outline shimmering. Its metal burning. Its plastic seat melting. Damp air from the turned soil rises and steams away like the surface of a tea-cup. The soil's skin is dry and tight; but underneath is raw flesh. Everything is still. Everything waits. Unseen, the cuckoo moves on. In the hedge a tiny sparrow sits innocently on a single massive egg.

The school bell rings the end of the day. Penny rushes because she wants to get home, have a bath, get changed so she can casually meet the bulldozer driver in the field. She is pleased to see that it is at the far side, facing the other way. She doesn't want to be seen yet with ink on her fingers and her second-best socks. She scuttles along the hedge, her satchel bulging. She has a history essay to do tonight. She'll do it afterwards. The cuckoos call is louder as the air grows weary of the day.

Passing Teresa's hot bungalow, where every window is sealed like blind eyes, Penny notices that two milk bottles still stand on the doorstep. That's not like Teresa. She picks them up. They are hot, the contents as thick as cheese. She rings the bell. There is no reply. She is about to turn when she hears a low moan.

She knows her mother has the spare key. Her mother has all the neighbours' keys as chairperson of the Fieldview Neighbourhood Watch. She flings her satchel on the kitchen floor and scours the house for her mother. There is a note on the hall-stand. 'Gone shopping. Sausages in fridge. Don't take all the milk. And No Mess.' Two flies batter against the window. Outside the cuckoo still calls. The air is as thick as the milk on the doorstep. It curdles.

Penny holds her breath when she eventually forces Teresa's door. It is sealed with old newspapers. The hall smells of rancid mince. The air is clotted. Teresa is huddled in the middle of the lounge floor, her skirt held protectively around her bare ankles. Her feet are stained with blood. The carpet is wet. She rocks backwards and forwards. 'Cuckoo. Cuckoo,' she calls plaintively as if to a lover. She smiles.

Penny looks around her. She runs along the hall to the box-room she knows from her mother has yellow teddy-bear wallpaper and new lace curtains. The cot is white and empty. She runs back to Teresa. 'Where's the baby? Have you had it? Have you called the doctor? What about an ambulance?'

Teresa croons. 'Cuckoo. Cuckoo.'

The cuckoo outside slows its call like a clockwork toy whose spring is slowly winding down. Penny glances at the violated cow-field and sees the bulldozer silent and driverless. She still has time to get herself ready to meet her new lover. Her first lover. She will float through the cow-field, the fronds of meadow-parsley will brush her arms like finger-tips. Only she must get help. Try Sadie. She's a kind sort.

Sadie's door is unlocked. Follow Penny from room to empty room. The house is neat and pink like a Wendy house. There are china cottages on the window-sills. A plastic ballerina pirouettes, one pink toe teetering on the edge of an onyx ash-tray. There are two half-empty glasses in the kitchen. The tap drips. She smells cigarette smoke and what her mother calls cheap scent. As she pushes the bedroom door she hears a soft moan. Is everyone bewitched? Is it the sun? The heat? The throb of the bulldozer? The call of the cuckoo? Has everyone gone to the moon?

On the bed two bodies move slowly and rhythmically like the bulldozer lifting and lowering its huge arm across the red-soil gashes of the cowfield. The man's back is brown and sheened in a film of sweat. The muscles in his shoulder ripple like shook velvet. Sadie sees Penny transfixed in the doorway. She screams. The bulldozer driver pulls away from her palpating baby flesh. 'What the shit?' Then he grins. 'Oh, it's only the school-kid. Now, where was I?' Sadie laughs as she disappears beneath the muscle.

The air is cooler now, streaked mauve at the edges, fading like a bruise. The bulldozer stands proudly in the middle of the field it has laid to waste, awaiting its transport home. The cuckoo is somewhere and is silent at last. The ambulance screams away from Fieldview Crescent, its blue light a brisk bustle of officialdom. Geoff follows, grim and grey, in the police car. They found the baby behind the hardboard in the cold fireplace, its baby-bird mouth stuffed with newspaper.

Penny is curled in her bed, a pillow stuffed into her mouth to stifle the stupid sobs that will not stop. Is this life? Is this where her education is leading her? To men who prefer the old tired flesh of Sadie to the bouncing thighs of promising, blooming youth? To women who murder their babies? To fields where cows once waded up to their bellies in soft, damp grass now crushed to support houses for new Sadies, new Teresas and Geoffs and all the rest who see nothing because they are too busy buying another pair of shoes?

Sadie sleeps. She finished the bottle of gin alone. Washed the bulldozer driver from between her legs and stretched out in blissful talcum-powdered peace. She loves sleeping alone. It's the daylight that terrifies her. It knows too much. Two pink bunny slippers wait for morning when the cuckoo will be wound up and ready to go.

In the darkness beyond, beneath the ash-tree at the bottom of Penny's garden where the cuckoo sleeps, a bat swoops low on soft grey wings, whispering with dark and secret purpose like leaves before a storm.

QUINQUIREME

The wind whips a skipping rope of hair across my face. *Salt, mustard, vinegar, pepper. Bubble gum, Bubble Gum. What do you wish?* The vehicles roar down the hill like the wolf on the fold, their cohorts gleaming in purple and gold… until the lights change and I smell salt and seaweed although the city is miles away from the ocean.

'Quinquireme?' my head of department spat. 'Old-fashioned elitism. You can't expect kids to relate to that.' I shrug. Feel the words, roll them round until the edges are smooth, *Qinquireme of Ninevah. Topazes and cinnamon and gold moidores.*

Put out to grass. I swing my bag of books up the hill to where the old oak shades the bus, and off we go.

The bus swings past the Polly Garter terraces, gardens that grow washing and babies. When Mark was three I soothed him with words. *It is spring, moonless night, in the small town, silent and bible-black…* and off he'd sail into sleep.

He works in wood. Broad as an oak, sinews like saplings, soft as sawdust and poetry. *Sandalwood, cedarwood and sweet white wine.* Mark drinks Real Ale, dark and malty, rich as amber.

I took my classes to that oak before half of it split away. Robin Hood slept in this oak, I told them. See! There's Merlin curled in the silver birch. Listen! Listen to its leaves. You don't have to understand poetry to hear the rhythm of words and wood.

The bus sails on, stately Spanish galleon rising on the crest of the by-pass. The wind picks up, tossing the seagulls over the roof-tops like torn scraps of silver foil – and oh!

My bag falls onto the floor. I straighten up. The world has splintered into blocks of wood. Children's bricks of solid images scattered across the floor. *Sandalwood, cedarwood, sweet white wine*. Outside, a stiff man, scarf horizontal in the silent wind, freezes on one end of a lead attached to a wooden dog. That woman, her mouth, an open letter-box of laughter, is at the door, her arm a branch scratching the bell. The frayed man with a carved ponytail on the seat in front, dandruff like sawdust on his collar, stares, his face a chiselled gargoyle.

I lift my arm, my bag solid as my mother's mahogany sideboard. The bus is now empty of all but the driver, a cigarette in his mouth, the smoke a thumbed smudge.

More people. Wooden people. Painted clothes, uniforms. Tinker, tailor, soldier, sailor, rich man, policeman, paramedic, nurse…

I am in a bed. Mark is here. I feel the softness of cloth, the whisper of a heart, the tang of new wood, spicy as ginger. The warmth of a son. *Topazes and cinnamon and gold moidores.*

Don't speak Mum. But I do. *Ivory and apes and peacocks*.

He leans into my mouth. Picks up the words: *Firewood, iron-ware and cheap tin trays*.

SHE SELLS SEA SHELLS

I am a curiosity. Whispers follow me, shadow me down the Church Cliffs and Black Ven; they swirl around me, then are snatched by the wind that sweeps Lyme Bay where I work, hammer in hand. Sniggers are hidden in pocket handkerchiefs, muffled by bonnets, stifled like the squeals of unwanted puppies and kittens stuffed into sacks and hurled from the Cobb at high-tide at midnight.

Winter squats on the thatch, drips through the eaves, runs down the walls where black mould trickles. Outside, the sun is metal-bright but the wind howls down the chimney, sneaks through the latch. Outside the church clock is stuck, time frozen between its hands. Inside, Mother hugs the fire, bundled in shawls, her back curved away from me.

'So another gentleman slips through your net.' She nods to the newspaper that lies between us. She spits into the flames. They hiss but I say nothing. I write my notes, read my books. The candle writhes and gutters. I blow on my fingers.

'Thought you were off to London.'

I throw down my pen. My rage will not be confined. It needs space to roar.

This morning I saw the newspaper, its torn wings flapping in the gutter. I picked it up. It was a month old, frayed at the edges, beer-stained, well-thumbed by greasy fingers. I took it home to enjoy at my leisure until Mother snatched it from me, poked a bony finger at the illustration. 'Isn't that your young man, Mary? Such a handsome fellow. All girls were in a flutter when he was here.'

'Not me, Mother.'

'So, why's he in the papers, Mary? Tell me. He must have done something special.' She can out-talk and out-drink sailors, utter more profanities than the King's troopers and beat any Excise man in a sneering contest but can neither read nor write. Never taught herself as I did from newsprint wrapped round fish-heads or washed up at high-tide jumbled with rope and rotted timber, old bottles and lamp-oil. Waste of time. What's the use of book-learning? You've been touched by the sun, Mary. You're not right in the head.

Now it is afternoon. The light is all but gone but his eyes pierce the darkness from the page and my mother's taunts are as sharp as a crab's pinch.

I pull my cloak and bag from the peg. 'And shut the door behind you,' she screams, matching the wind that flows in to take my place. I take the hammer from my bag. The sea doesn't stop revealing its secrets just because there's no-one to see it. We are nothing to the rocks that mark our passing. Philip said that millions of years hence our bones would be discovered on a mountain's summit. They will call them snakestones, devil's fingers, verteberries, cupid's wings. That's what the visitors call them. That's what they'll be wanting when the spring comes. Curiosities.

What do they do with them, these fragments of Genesis; relics from the Flood? Lock them under glass domes on their mantelpieces for their maids to dust?

When he came it was summer and my table was piled high with curiosities; snakestones that are ammonites; belemnites they call the devil's fingers. I made a tidy sum that season although money is poor recompense. I am thankful for the meat that feeds my belly and the coal that nourishes the fire. It is my mind that starves.

Now it is winter; the table is bare and my heart is stone; the fossilized remains of hope buried deep in the earth, scoured by the tides of a thousand oceans, shattered by a thousand frosts; blasted by a thousand winds. A curiosity.

I wasn't the first Mary my mother bore. She toddled into the fire when she was two. I inherited the name but neither her looks nor her sunny disposition as Mother is often wont to remind me. I am benighted, a child of the elements, who did not speak until a freak bolt of lightning skewered me to the earth. The next day, I found my very first ammonite, as round as a cart-wheel. A lady bought it for half a crown. A fortune to me until my first true find earned me twenty sovereigns. The clever men pored and picked over every bone and decided it was something new but centuries old. A paradox that calls the Bible into question. A mystery. A challenge. And I found it, over yonder see? Where that buttress of shale extends a nervous toe into the icy foam. It is now preserved behind glass, sleepy, drowsy with beeswax and curious eyes stare and do not understand even though it now has a name. *Teleosaurus chapmani*; named after the man who bought it from me and told the world he'd found it.

Today the shore is as cold and hard as stone and I am here alone. Do not pity me for I relish my solitude. Today the sun dazzles a crystalline sky and the cliffs are glazed and fissured, battered by the high, relentless waves. On softer days when clouds bulge like soot-filled sacks and the shore is ink-black, a shaft of light will break free and strike one facet of the rock I have seen a hundred times. Yet in that second, there it is, as clear as blown crystal, the skeleton of a new beast and I am the first to see it since the day it died and sank into the mud of a tropical sea and began to turn to stone.

In early spring, when the sun is young and the tide is high, the sea is kittenish and licks the shale from the foot of the cliff. The breeze is soft on my cheeks and swells my skirts like sails. The sun is on my back and my bare feet curl around warmed pebbles and tepid pools. I fly from rock to rock but my eye never wavers. In summer, others share the shoreline with me, turning over rocks, raking the pools, but they haven't my eye. That's why they all need me, these clever men. That's why he clung to me and I was glad. His grateful smile cradled me in its warmth.

Mother fussed about him when he first came; pushed him into the inglenook and forced a jug of ale on him. He couldn't be held. He was coiled tight with curiosity and ambition. He was young, broad-shouldered as a plough-boy, as tanned as a sailor.

I led him down to the shore. The path zigzags back on itself as it clings to the cliff. Uneven slabs of stone tip this way and that, worn like old teeth by the tramp of cocklewomen, foragers and fishermen and slick with gull-shit.

He was not the first gentleman to seek me out. They wash in and out like dead crabs on the tide. But of all the men who have betrayed me, it is his brains I would take most pleasure in splattering across the rocks. His name was Philip Field. A soft name, as soft as his fair hair that fell to his shoulders and streamed in the wind like a banner. He was forever brushing it from his face. I can see him now, the sun proud behind him, laughing at what we had found. Laughing because in our triumph we were as one in our joy.

He was a chattering magpie by nature, I taught him silence. When one visit became three, then five and he and I were focused on our task, he never uttered a word but shared my eyes as I scanned for recent slips and slides and picked out a fresh slice of exposed bluff, raw as flesh. We walked for hours, days. The weeks were strung like shining beads along a silver skein. We waded the waves, jumped the clefts careless of the water boiling beneath us. We tramped the sands, skirted the cliffs, climbing up, clambering, bouldering, falling and laughing, scrambling in the mud, sliding down, catching and crawling, up and across and down and over until the sun grew bored and left us to the stars. Our backs and legs ached, our arms were heavy, our eyes stinging with scouring the miles of rock, most times dun, sometimes blue, most times grey, seeking the slightest alteration in the contours in the hard light of sea and sky, the salt, the tin-foil flash of the birds above our head, reflected in the wet sand puddled around our feet.

From time to time he stopped, caught my arm and pointed. 'Look! There! Can you see?' And I would shake my head and his eyes would fade from blue to grey to disappointment and on we plodded. My head ached to please him, to see the blue return.

One day a sudden storm roared in from the Channel and caught us in its fury. The birds fled. The waves roared and hurled themselves at the cliffs like dogs at the end of their chains. The wind ripped the shale from the slopes. It rattled like gunfire. The rain sliced our cheeks and soaked our clothes.

As we clung together to withstand the onslaught, a slab of the eastern headland collapsed. It began with a rumble which he thought was thunder. He gripped my hand. It was strong but as softly warm in my palm as a dog's muzzle. We stood in silent awe as the slab, as wide as the harbour wall, subsided like a lady's curtsey and settled at the foot of the cliff in a flurry of flounces and lace. That's how he described it later but I didn't see what he meant, not knowing of ladies' curtseys, lace or flounces.

We waited, too terrified to breathe, our clothes plastered to our limbs, hair dripping like kelp. The storm passed. The sun peered through the streaming tatters of retreating cloud and the birds returned to feast on the flapping fishes gasping on the sand. Then he whispered, his mouth touching my ear. 'Do you think? Could there possibly be?'

I looked and truth to say I prayed, although I know that God is man's invention for what he doesn't understand.

He was so close to me he felt my body stiffen. 'What, where?' he cried, 'I can't see.' The wind grew as impatient with him as I and once more began its torments, tugging at his coat tails, tearing his hat from his hand and giving it wings. He brushed his hair from his face in the way that was no as familiar to me as my own hand. He looked like a child who had lost his mother.

My feet were drowning in my boots. 'We must go,' I said, 'before the tide cuts us off.' I urged him back to the town.

'You've seen something. I know you have,' he said, dancing like the boy who has found his mother, all his fear forgotten in her angry face.

I didn't tell him what I had seen. Not then. One word too soon and every fool is out with his pickaxe. This was mine and it would stay mine.

'Meet me at low tide tomorrow,' I said before we parted in the street. I saw curious eyes. I didn't care.

God still smiled on me then for the next day we had the shore to ourselves. I felt his breath close to mine as we laboured to release the beast from its rocky cage. We touched a rib, a toe bone and a long snout. We trembled with the newness of it, that we alone in all the world could see it and learn its secrets. When our hands and arms were too weak to dig further, we fashioned the beast on paper, took measurements, made notes. Fingers numb, wrapped in cloth, we worked. He is university-taught and his pen is fine. His drawings are exquisite, shaded with unsurpassed delicacy to give shape and form but retain clarity. I peered over his shoulder to learn his craft. That night I toiled, copying his simple lines until the fire was out and dawn came. His sketches are published; his notes in print. Mine are under my bed, curling at the edges, rotting.

Day after day we returned. I took care to take my bag

and bring it back brimming with the usual fare; the verteberries and the snake-stones to keep the fire burning and curious tongues still.

On the hottest day of that summer we had dug and scraped, teased and coaxed all morning until exhaustion overcame us and we lay on the beach, our faces to the sky our backs to the hot sand. The silence was companionable; the seagulls' cries a lullaby. When I woke he was sitting up and making more sketches in his fine leather-bound journal. 'I am so excited, Mary,' he said, his breath coming in short rasps. 'It's something completely new,' he added, his pen scratching the paper, his knuckles white as he wrestled with the wind for its possession. 'Can you see,' he said, as if I hadn't seen it first, 'the line of the jaw, the way the front limb articulates, the uneven number of teeth? Do you think we can lift it soon? Do you think we can do it without help?' He was anxious, his body a jangling wire, his head turning this way and that. 'I don't want a soul to know. It's only you I trust.'

'We cannot lift it alone,' I said, hugging his faith in me close lest it fly away. 'But I know a man who will not talk.'

'Oh, Mary,' he cheered. 'You are a wonderful. What would I do without…' He paused and the greedy wind snatched the words from his mouth and tossed them into the sea where they drowned. Too late for I had heard them. As quick as mercury, he caught me in his arms. And it was good and warmer than summer and I trembled with the newness of it. And he took my face in his hands and kissed me, murmuring, 'I will never forget this moment. Never. I will blow the world apart with my discovery!'

I pushed him away, seized his pen from the sand and hurled it in the air where it landed, nib down, in a pool. He grabbed me by the waist. 'Oh you tease! You wanton woman!' he cried his head back, bloated with laughter.

'It's *our* discovery!' I cried. In one beat of my heart I saw grey steel sharpen his eyes before the blue returned and he twirled me round and round until I was dizzy. Was this flirtation? If it was, then it was not what I desired. I pulled away.

'*Ours*,' I said.

His face softened. He caught my face in my hand and stroked my salty cheek with the back of his finger. 'Of course. Mary. Our discovery,' he whispered. Then he kissed me again. Hard. Harder. I felt his weight on my shoulder, urging me to the soft sand. 'Mary, Mary,' he groaned. His lips teased mine and I began to see why the other girls long for the touch and smell of a man. I softened, my knees melted and he filled me with his beauty.

'Ours,' screeched a gull arcing above us. 'Ours!'

I know what you're thinking. That I am no better than the others, my head turned by a man's easy attention. But that is not what made my knees melt and released my soul to the heavens. Aye, I believed in Heaven at that moment. It was our Heaven and we had made it. Together we had made a great discovery and the world was about to open for us like a flower after rain.

What a fool; a greater fool than Becky White who was left belly full after she'd crowed that her sea-captain was taking her back to his Russian palace. Her laughter died when the black ship left without her and she was brought to bed in the Poor House. Even though she was married off to Tom Fowler, loudmouthed and loathsome, free with his fists but tight with his pennies, even she tilts her nose at me as she shuffles by, another child grizzling in her arms, four more clinging to her muddy petticoats.

Even she knows; knows that our discovery now has a name. *Teleosaurus Fielderi*. The newspaper is burned but the words will never leave me. 'Discovered on the Dorset coast by the distinguished geologist, Mr Philip Field.' The eyes that looked up from the page were as bright as ever but his face was drawn inward beneath a new-grown beard as befits a celebrated and learned fellow of the Royal Geological Society.

'Mr Philip Field accepted the accolades of his fellows at a special dinner held in his honour in London last week. This popular young man was, in his gracious and elegantly expressed reply, fulsome in his praise of his fellow learned gentlemen who had seen fit to elevate him to their illustrious ranks. He then held his audience in thrall as he related how, after days of solitary toil, his keen eye discovered this most curious of creatures.'

I wander back along the foreshore, plucking a snakestone here, an angel's wing there. I will slice some salt pork and boil potatoes for supper and prepare Mother for bed. I will read my books until my candle dies and then, come dawn, will take my hammer and bag to the shore. In spring I will once more set up my table of curiosities outside our door. Day will follow day until my bones are laid in the ground and someone else digs them up. They will preserve me behind glass and put someone else's name beneath my fossilized remains. People will flock to visit me. A strange, rare and interesting object. A curiosity.

WAITING FOR THE BUS

It is six o'clock and the day is tired and dirty. The wind funnels a steady torrent of trucks, taxis, bikes, motorbikes, vans, buses both single and double-decker, cars and yet more cars up the hill. Blue exhaust splutters into faces, greasing hair and dulling the complexion. Eddies of dead leaves are dragged tumbling like filthy kite-tails along the pavement, gathering paper cups, drinks cans and newspaper.

A bus squeals to a halt opposite the Odeon. The doors rattle open, swallow the queue, disgorge the rejects, rattle closed. The bus picks up speed, shudders, brakes, swerves to avoid a delivery van that has cut in front of it then growls away up the hill.

The bus doors have rattled closed in Maureen Miller's face. She has missed the bus by the skin of her teeth – the skin of her sodding teeth, having wobbled on weak ankles all the way from the tube station. Her shoes pinch and her tights – new on that morning for the interview for the job she didn't get, have been snagged by a belligerent shopping basket. She watches in impotent rage as the bus sails serenely up the hill and away, scooped into the sweep of the traffic, roaring off into the murky-brown city sunset. So much for a long soak in the tub. That Romanian in the downstairs room will have got in first, leaving curled black pubic hairs clogging the plug-hole and a tide mark as wide as an oil-slick – and cold water. At least she's first in the queue. Another bus will come in about three minutes if she's lucky.

Glenda Green in her frayed anorak and pull-on hat that date back to her Greenham Common days arrives at the stop, sniffs disapprovingly at the girl in front of her. Short-skirt, sling-backed shoes, diamante buckles, heels as high as a skyscraper. Has twenty years' struggle to free her sisters from body slavery done nothing? Where is that bus?

The timetable says every three minutes between four-thirty and seven. What a joke. And whose fault is that? Glenda knows. It's the Tories who call themselves New Labour. Whatever happened to proper socialism?

No sign of a bus. Six minutes have passed. Shaz is still crying as she drags Dougie to the end of the small queue. Dougie drops an awkward arm on her shoulder. Shaz pushes it away. 'This is all your fault. You didn't remind me to take my pill.' Dougie grins but doesn't let her see. He has fathered a child. Scored the winning goal. He kicks an empty Starbucks cup in triumph. It catches the legs of the woman in front of him, an anonymous back in a filthy old anorak. She turns round sharply and scowls. Dougie doesn't care. He's going to be a father. He's going down the Feathers tonight to crow to the boys. They'll be well-impressed – that is, if this fucking bus will ever come and Shaz will shut up. He always thought women wanted kids. Not bloody Shaz. Has to be different, don't she? But he's got to stick with her now if he ever wants to take his kid to the Emirates Stadium to see the lads in action. Reckon he can put up with Shaz for that.

It is five minutes since the last bus. George Ferris carefully places himself a yard behind the couple in front, who look decidedly common, and pretends he isn't waiting for a bus, but idly passing the time. A gentleman of leisure. He flips open his mobile. 'Yeah. Right. Bit busy at the mo. Cheers, he says to no-one. Now the day is over at Madame for Fashion, Oxford Street, he can pretend he doesn't spend his day mouthing platitudes to sweaty fat ladies in front of flattering mirrors, pretending that the thin polyester they pour their bulk into suits them. He smoothes his hand over his bald head and anticipates the evening ahead. His bath will be run, soft towels aired. Mario will have the dinner in the oven and will be ready with the oils. Such an obliging boy. One day when he's old enough George will buy him his own little run-around, one of those sweet little blue Fiats with dimpled curves like Mario's sweet little arse. Then he won't have to slum it on public transport, although sometimes there's the chance to catch the eye of a darling boy and invite him home for an old-fashioned English tea with afters when Mario's at his English class. George prefers Greek boys but Mario from Palermo will to do for the time being. Such a sweet, obliging boy. He flocks open his phone. 'Yeah. Hi! Returning your call. About those shares,' he says to the dialling tone.

It is fifteen minutes since the last bus. Suddenly the queue is dazzled by the blast of blue and white light as an ambulance roars past, scattering traffic, filling heads with the scream of its siren that changes pitch as it roars past. The Doppler Effect remembers Anne joining the queue behind a fat man, wheezing platitudes into his mobile – a walking coronary if ever there was one. She rests two bulging carrier bags on the pavement either side of her thick sensible ankles and idly watches the ambulance pass, relieved it has nothing to do with her. The Doppler effect, she smiles. Fancy remembering that. She hasn't thought of such things since third year physics with Mr Schofield and his soft brown eyes and endearing blush for whom she wore black bras beneath her white school shirt. She's glad he never seemed to notice though.

Lucky baby, languorous in the warm waters of my belly thinks Sunetra, joining the tail of the long, long queue behind the English woman and her two carrier bags full of easy convenience food she is not allowed to buy. Lucky English woman. Your back doesn't ache, your head doesn't pound with the thud of the treadle, the grind of the wheel, the stab of the needle through shirt after shirt after shirt. Who needs all these cheap shirts? Tonight I will spend hours cooking for a dull husband and a mother-in-law who will despise me even more deeply if you, my precious baby, turn out to be a girl. Oh to be alone, languorous in warm water, turning slowly, floating, drifting around the dark silent softness of the universe, stretched, sleeping, sleeping forever, forever…

'Quick!' calls Mum, pacing the traffic up the hill, towing Sophie by the tug of her arm. 'Quick!' repeats Sophie to Mr Ted, his one remaining brown ear scrunched in her other hand.

The bus is coming!' cries Mum to Sophie.

'The bus is coming,' cries Sophie to Mr Ted.

'Let the others get on first, love.' She smiles at the Indian girl in front. So serene they are, so sure of themselves in their elegant saris and smooth black hair. They could teach us a thing or two.

'Aren't we lucky?' says Mum as the queue shuffles forward and Mum hoists Sophie and Mr Ted up the steps of the big red bus, fumbling in her bag for change before the doors hwish shut.

Mum lifts Sophie on to her knee and Sophie sits Mr Ted on hers so that he can drive the big red bus up the hill. As he steers the bus away from the stop, Kate turns round and sees the man who has just missed it jumping up and down and waving. She and Mr Ted wave back as the big, red bus sails away into the sunset and fish fingers on toast, her favourite.

It's fifteen minutes to the next bus. Tony swears and pulls a dog-eared copy of *The Da Vinci Code* from his pocket and continues where he left off.

SAILING TO BYZANTIUM

If only she'd arrived by sea, hauled her boat up on the silver sands and walked barefoot into the city, bringing nothing with her but the pearls of sea-water dripping from her toes.

If only her first view of the shore had been a violet smudge in the blue, the crown of slender white minarets circling the city like birthday candles, her own music would have chimed with the melody this city had sung forever. Then, she would have left her world behind and sailed across the seas, allowing her body to tune to another beat, to tie a stone to her guilt and hurl it into the silver waters.

Instead, she caught a flight from Gatwick and landed at the airport, was whisked along traffic-choked roads in an air-conditioned coach that roared through Constantine's walls and dropped her at a hotel, where everyone spoke English and the wine was French.

She was shown to her room. She kicked off her shoes. Pressing her cheek against the cool glass she watched a flaming red sky fade behind the forest of silhouetted minarets to mauve, then grey. The call to prayer mocked her in its intensity. She showered and slipped into bed, where she slept only fitfully. The bed was too large.

The following day she felt she had to explore the city she didn't want to see. Jack was like a tooth that continued to ache long after it had been removed; his absence a hollow her tongue had to probe, again and again until her gum was sore. He was with her in the Grand Bazaar where, had he been alive, he would have pointed out the sacks of saffron, cinnamon and a hundred spices she couldn't name. He would have laughed at the couple who bought a plastic camel made in Taiwan. He would have known where to buy cheap tickets to cruise the Bosphorus, not the tourist package she found. She knew, that by handing over a pile of notes she couldn't be bothered to count to the men on the dockside, she had been foolish. She could feel their scorn burning her back as she crossed the fragile plank between shore and ship wishing she could run away, catch the next flight home, knowing she couldn't.

It was almost midday and the sun a high lantern before the boat swung away from the crowded quay and headed off into the steamy haze. In the diamond dazzle of the sun on the water distant ships moved like black paper cut-outs against a backdrop of tin-foil. She left the huddled knot around their guide and went to the other side of the boat and leaned over the rail, tasting salt and oil in the spray.

What would Jack have done? He wouldn't, like the man next to her in a Hawaiian shirt, have listed aloud the 'must-see' sites and counted the red stars, too intent on the page to see and feel them. His arm resting gently on her shoulder, he would have told her tales about Jason and his brave Argonauts and their heroic quest to bring back the Golden Fleece. He would have explained that the route from Thessaly to Colchis would have brought them through these very waters. He would have filled her with wonder and magic. And then, she would not have seen the rusted hulks of Russian tankers plodding back and forth to the Black Sea, but heard Orpheus's sweet voice urging the men forward, their oars flinging up glittering necklaces of water with every stroke.

The boat chugged on, churning up scum and twenty-first century flotsam, trailing a greasy wake along the shore before tying up alongside a group of weather-boarded houses. She vaguely remembered the 'Fine Feast included in Price' and found herself at the tail of an obedient gaggle filing into a garish Arabesque establishment, its menu splashed in every language except Turkish. They were immediately accosted by a barrage of hawkers pressing on all sides. Children scampered around them like eager puppies, thrusting roses and fans of postcards into their faces, rattling fabric birds on wooden sticks.

A small boy tugged her sleeve. She looked down into a pair of enormous sable eyes and a shy grin. She fumbled in her bag. The man with the guide-book forced his way between them and, grabbing her shoulders, pushed her into the restaurant where the party was being squeezed onto wooden benches and offered a choice of Coca-Cola or Seven-Up. 'Don't you dare give those little money-grubbers any cash. You've got to show them who's boss or they'll walk all over you.'

She tightened her lips. 'Please excuse me,' she said and dived into the Ladies.

She splashed her blazing face in water. She raged with impotent anger. Not at the interfering man who had meant well. The cooling water replaced her hot anger with memories that made her shiver. As a young widow, her position at the usual obsequies was assured. People wrote her letters edged in black about sorrow and loss. People she didn't know turned to her with appropriately mournful faces when she entered the chapel where Jack lay in a box smothered in white lilies.

Her face was a perfect mask and everyone nodded and touched her shoulder. She had taken her place in the front pew, dry eyed and composed and remained still as the curtains had closed and the recorded organ piped out a piece of Bach that Jack had always hated. She almost smiled – Jack's lips would have twitched wickedly – but knew that if she had done so, she would have begun to laugh and never stop.

The day of Jack's funeral had been hideous from beginning to end. Jack's mother embraced her when she left, enveloping her in lavender and saintliness. 'The tears will come,' she said, 'when you least expect them. Don't waste the tickets. Take that holiday and think of Jack.'

It was hard not to.

He'd brought the tickets home the same day she'd found a grubby lace handkerchief in his pocket. It was the corniest scenario ever. She had been emptying the pockets of one of his work jackets. They needed frequent cleaning. From the amount of chalk ground into the seams, she used to tease, anyone would think he used them as blackboard dusters.

She should have tackled him the moment he came home. But he was too excited about his long-dreamed visit to Istanbul. Had she done so, he would have squashed her accusations with a laugh, pulled her to him and kissed away her anger. The truth was as simple as a child's story. An evening spent with a female colleague had been exactly what he said it was; a chance to plan next term's timetable away from the distractions of the staff-room. The woman, a cart-horse of un-coordination, had knocked over a mug of tea and pulled out her handkerchief to mop it up. When the meeting was over, Jack had swept it up absent-mindedly.

The woman came to the funeral. Miss Nugent, head of the History department and old enough to be Jack's mother bore down on her, a glass of sweet sherry in her hand and after the usual 'such a waste of a promising young teacher, so tragic etc.' she added, 'I hope you didn't mind me taking up so much of his time last month, picking his brain over timetabling. He was so good at that sort of thing. I'm hopeless,' she had added, waving her arms about, sherry droplets flying through the air. 'Disorganized,' she laughed, 'and clumsy,' she added, knocking over a chair as she backed away.

So simple. So idiotically banal. How could she have

concocted a sordid tale of adultery out of that? It was laughable. But she hadn't laughed then. She'd given Jack the silent treatment, turned her back in bed, gritted her teeth as he talked dreamily of Istanbul and its layer upon layer of history. 'Did you know,' he said one night, 'that the horses of Saint Marks were stolen from Constantinople as trophies of war?'

'Amazing,' she said, leafing the pages of her magazine, letting jealousy eat away her flesh and scrape her bones. He looked at her. She looked away.

Following an exchange of angry words at breakfast over nothing Jack had slammed out of the house only to be run over by a speeding taxi on his way to school, his inattention no doubt due to his distraction.

What a mess. And here she was, where she didn't want to be as it was his dream, adding her guilt and her shame to the layers of this city. Constantinople, Byzantium, Istanbul.

How many shattered dreams lay crumbled in its dust?

The street was quiet as she slipped out of the restaurant; the children had gone to sell their trinkets elsewhere. Small birds fluttered from the almond trees. She turned her face to the sparkling waters criss-crossed by tacking yachts and there, amongst them she thought she caught a glimpse of the Argo and its crew pulling on the ropes, their sun-blackened faces glistening with sweat. And was that Heracles scanning the shore and Orpheus strumming his lyre as the waters lilted past and fishes leapt to the beat of the drum that set the stroke of the oars? A tanker crossed her eye line, booming on its way to the Black Sea, dimming the sun.

She trailed along the street, hugging the shade, turned one corner, then another, not caring where she was headed. Ahead of her was an old crumbling mosque. Trees rooted in the arches; weeds climbed the walls. She wanted to know why it had been abandoned but there was no-one to ask. Jack would have known. Jack would have eased her into this city, so that she would have slipped into its time and moved through it. Nothing made sense. Old men shuffled past, their faces as wizened as walnuts, their backs doubled under huge bales of fabric. Where were they going and why? Handcarts piled high with shirts wobbled in and out of the crowds. Men sat in doorways, playing cards, drinking apple tea, smoking thin cigarettes. What did they talk about? On she trudged, wishing she'd had the sense not to wear silly strappy sandals. She climbed endless flights of stone stairs, tripped over broken paving slabs until she was hot, dizzy and totally lost. She had been stupid to leave the restaurant without eating something. She had been stupid to even think of taking Jack's holiday alone. She sank onto a stone wall and took off a sandal, rubbed her heel. A blister had formed, red and hot, soft as jelly to her probing fingers. Stupid. Stupid.

She looked up to find she had become an object of intrigue. Men had stopped and were eyeing her curiously as if she was a kingfisher who had landed in a flock of starlings. Keep calm. Keep calm. What was it Jack used to say? If you don't know where you are, fix your eyes on a familiar landmark and walk towards it in as straight a line as possible.

She remembered that her hotel faced two of the most famous buildings in Istanbul. Hagia Sophia, once a Christian Church, then a mosque and now a museum, and the emblematic Blue Mosque faced each other across fountain-splashed gardens. She scanned the skyline and eventually saw their smoky shapes swimming on the horizon, took a deep breath and walked on. An hour or so later she arrived at the entrance to the Blue Mosque. She slipped off her sandals, set them on the rack and wound a scarf about her head. Lifting the heavy green curtain, she entered.

She had visited many great buildings with Jack. She had often been bored, although she'd never told him. She had trudged around them all: stately homes, castles, cathedrals, art-galleries, museums, until her body and her mind ached. They had ill-prepared her for this. She was overwhelmed, not merely by the coolness that fell around her. All large old buildings were cool. It wasn't that. No, it was the absolute sense of space. No pillars or chunks of masonry, no sombre tombs, no anguished statues, paintings or other representations of human agony; only light and lightness. All around her, she was conscious of the shimmer of the sea rippling in the blue-glassed windows. In the centre, beneath the gilded dome, a few men knelt, bowed, stood up and bowed again in prayer. Their faith was understated and therefore tangible, a soundless tableau. Man may have designed and constructed it but it transcended humanity.

Her eyes filled. She let the tears fall unchecked and cried until she was empty of pain and the light at the high windows had faded.

She stepped outside and put her shoes on again. The evening call to prayer burst across the evening sky. Seagulls rose in clouds from the minarets and wheeled about the golden cupolas, flashing silver. And the Argo slipped its mooring; its sails filled, rich and round, and sped away across the moonlit, glittering sea.

SKY TALKER

The night is as soft as a black bear's pelt and syrup thick. I am alone.

'You're Sky-Talker, yes?'

I scramble to my feet, fear swelling my throat. A man stands before me: Sharp-Spear, the chief's elder son, the fleetest of foot, the strongest of arm and the keenest of eye. Or was – until the day he slipped and plunged from the high cliffs into the big river, his body torn and broken. Now, he sleeps and sits by the fire with the women, carving bone needles and trinkets for barter. I see them sneer. What use is a man who cannot hunt?

'I am. That is the kindest name they call me.'

We remain silent. A shower of star-arrows streak across the heavens as swift as cats.

'The gods are hunting tonight,' I say. 'They will feast well.' Hunger and the memory of plenty gnaw my stomach.

'They are fortunate,' he says. 'It's all over for me.' Another bright arrow burns a path through the darkness. 'I have been watching you.'

And I watch him but I do not tell him this. 'Why is that?' I ask. 'Had your mighty father not spared me, I would have been taken at birth to the place of wind and stones and left to die. They say I am cursed. 'My limbs are too weak to cure a pelt or push a needle through leather. I fall to the ground. My eyes roll and my tongue babbles nonsense.'

'I have seen this.'

'You do yourself no good talking to me.'

I see shadows cloud his eyes. 'You're troubled,' I say. 'But take heart. You stood on the threshold of death. You could have drowned had your brother not dived into the river to save you.'

'Indeed. I owe him my life.' His lips are as taut as a bowstring.

I now understand. I have seen, when no one else sees, the way his brother looks at him; his eyes burning with hatred and jealousy. It is whispered that he was side by side with his brother when he fell. But men do not tell their stories to women nor do the women share their gossip with me.

'What does the sky tell you?' he asks.

So I speak of what I know and have told no-one before: that when the world sleeps I see aurochs, horses and bears in the stars and men with bows and arrows in pursuit. They stalk the beasts that gather by the sky rivers and I see the mighty winged horse rears up from the horizon when the first frosts of autumn touch the earth and watch it sink back when the leaves return to the trees, only to rise once more as the seasons turn. The heavens are restless. They are water running through my fingers; they tumble like a rock down a mountain and spin round and round like branches in a whirlpool. They tell me stories. 'Do you see,' I ask, 'the man with his pack of hunting dogs leaping over above the mountains? And that shining bull auroch over there with his females sheltering behind him? I know exactly where the sun will set when the grass begins to grow and where it will place itself when the blizzards roar down the plains, the ice river advances and the wolves' snouts are rimed with frost. I know when the moon will defy the sun and shadow his glory until he roars at her effrontery and she flees.'

I tell him how I long to learn all the secrets the sky withholds but the ice is too cruel in the long winter nights and the wolves too hungry and I retreat to the fire.

He says, 'What if I could bring the heavens inside the caves and fix them above your head so you could see them in the flicker of the flames?'

Surely he raves in madness? But his eyes are steady.

'I will use blood, crushed stones, charcoal and berry juice. Feathers and flint make more than arrows.'

'You will paint stories on the cave walls?' I ask, 'like the men paint their chests and faces before the Days of Sacrifice?'

Then, tears, as sharp as dogs' teeth, sting my eyes and mist the stars. 'Oh I see. You mock me. You despise me just like the others.

'You are wrong. We can do this together.'

'But your body will heal and you will hunt again. And you will be Chief.'

'I think not. My brother is impatient. He failed once but will not fail again. But until then… trust me.'

He takes my hand and places it on his heart. I feel its steady beat and I am no longer afraid.

SPLIT INFINITIES

Morag grabbed her purse and a coat from the rack by the door. She pushed her feet into the nearest pair of shoes and marched out from her flat into the grim reality of a damp and blustery night.

She seemed to remember there was a shop nearby that was always open. Not that she'd ever been in it. She didn't need 'convenience' stores. She never ran out of anything, let alone food for Pier Gynt and Solveig. But the moment she had got home she had reached into the fridge and found every shelf empty. Not just of the cats' dinner. Everything. No Caesar Salad, no yoghurt with bio-active enzymes, not even that bottle of 1982 Bordeaux Red. She couldn't understand it.

Now standing within the grubby confines of Rani's All-Nite Stores, rain dripping from her coat and forming puddles about her feet, she couldn't begin to fathom what she'd come in for. She had been working too hard. That's what it was. But at what exactly? She ran her own business she knew that much. But what exactly was it she did?

She wandered up and down the shelves. Bleach, soap, scouring pads. No that wasn't it. Something for dinner. People were coming round. But who? The store with its cracked concrete floor and 'Fine Wines for the Disserning Shopper', scrawled in black felt-tip on cardboard dangling at eye level appalled her. She hated dirt and disorder and loathed bad spelling. The place stank of earth and mouldy vegetables, but the cats were hungry. Cat food. That was it. Concentrate. She grabbed a large tin of something meaty and hurried to the checkout. Delving into her coat pocket out fell a grubby handkerchief screwed up with a five pound note. Where was her purse?

The man behind the counter accepted the note with a

toothless smile. He wiped the dust from the top of the tin with his elbow and dropped it into a hideous canary-yellow carrier bag. No sooner had she stepped out onto the pavement than the handle broke and she found herself scrabbling in the gutter for the tin.

She was straightening up when a car screeched to a halt alongside her and the passenger door swung open.

'Hop in.'

She stared at him. She'd heard of kerb-crawlers but had never known they frequented this neighbourhood. Perhaps she ought to move. Thameside Villas was clearly no longer the best address in Maidenhead.

He spoke again. 'Hurry up, Mo! Neil will be arriving any minute and you said everything would be ready in good time.' He grinned. 'Mind you, you said that on our wedding day and even then you were half an hour late.'

The man was clearly mad. And yet he seemed familiar, his face as comfortable and warming as these old boots she never knew she had. An image; a name floated into her mind and fluttered away again. She had vague recollections of standing on a bridge contemplating her future when a young man with hair the colour of rope came sculling downstream. He had looked up at her and grinned. Why had she remembered such an irrelevant detail? Then a silly thought struck her. Had she allowed herself to get to know him she might not be here now. She might even have become some dowdy housewife in the suburbs. She'd never have become Morag Melville, who ran her own… ran her own what?

Somehow she found herself climbing into the car. She noted the rust under the door-sill with distaste. The springs sagged. Tins of paint and unboxed cassettes rolled about at her feet plus something squishy she didn't dare investigate. The car moved off with the roar and splutter of a clapped-out carburettor, the windscreen wipers wobbling in time to some tinny pop tune.

'So what you got us, then? I'm starving.'

Unable to articulate any of the inchoate thoughts tumbling around her head, she plunged her arm into Mr Rani's hideous yellow bag and fished out the tin. 'Pheasant in a Rich Red Wine Sauce,' she read aloud.

'Bloody Hell!' he laughed. 'Can we afford it? Mind you, this girl Neil's bringing might be the one and then we will be celebrating. The first of the kids to get off our hands. And the last. Can't see any one ever wanting to marry Gail, can you?'

She smiled weakly.

The car splashed on through the greasy back-streets. A monotonous succession of street-lamps zoomed past, each one exploding like a yellow firework then falling away, marking a step further from everything she knew. The more lamps she counted, the more she had to force herself to hang onto reality. She had two cats, but what were their names? Something Norwegian. So why did the ridiculous name, Pussikins, keep rising to the surface of her mind?

'Go away,' she muttered to the silly name. It slunk back into the shadows and stared at her balefully through narrowed eyes.

'First sign of madness, you know.'

'What?'

'Talking to yourself.'

That was it. She was going mad.

The windscreen wipers rocked. Her head reeled. The music rolled. 'Do I know this tune? It's awfully familiar.' The man grinned but said nothing. She wanted to hit him.

They came to a roundabout and he slowed down. Here the street-lamps changed from sodium yellow which distorted everything in their glow to a more realistic white. This was her first chance to examine him properly. He was about the same age as her, about forty, reasonably slim, but with the beginnings of a paunch. He had probably been handsome once and although he wasn't by any means bald, his hair line was creeping away from his forehead. She imagined that it was once the texture and colour of rope, the sort you tie up boats with…

She must have gasped. The man turned. Concerned. 'You Okay?'

She swallowed and nodded, but she wasn't. She could remember running her fingers through such hair. When? It was a long time ago. He was young. She was young. They were lying together looking up at a blue sky peeping through a canopy of overlapping leaves, golden-tipped with sunlight. She was happy. She loved him. She knew his name.

'Tim Frazer!' she cried out.

'Now what have I done?'

'Nothing.' She tucked her head inside her raincoat and the journey continued in silence.

They were driving along a suburban road of identical Tudor-gabled houses. He signalled too late, braked too late and swung left almost colliding with a pair of battered gates. He may have missed this time, but judging from the rusting dents that pock-marked the posts, he wasn't always as successful.

A light flashed on from behind the glass-paned front door. A teenage girl emerged. On her feet a pair of lop-eared rabbit slippers; on her face, the obligatory teenage scowl. 'What took you so long? Neil's phoned. Said they'll be here in ten minutes. Pussikins is being a right pain. There's no crisps and I'm starving. Honestly, Mum! How could you forget to go shopping? You must be going senile.'

'Don't speak to your mother like that! Come back this minute! Gail!' An upstairs door slammed shut.

'Feeling better after a good night's sleep?'

She opened her eyes a fraction and found the strange man bending over her with a mug of strong tea with 'The World's Best Mum' printed on it.

Oh for a china cup of Lapsang Suchong, she pleaded silently. She had also been hoping that when she woke she would find it had all been a dream, like in one of those awful TV soaps she never watched.

She took a cautious sip. The tea wasn't as bad as she had feared. She drained the mug.

'Want another?' She shook her head.

'It's not like you to refuse a top-up. Sure you're okay? You weren't yourself last night. A bit quiet. Shall I make you an appointment with Dr Jones?'

Again she shook her head.

'If you're sure. But take it easy today. I really have to get to work now, but phone me if you need me.'

'Of course,' she smiled. The sooner he was gone the better. Then she could leave. But what if she wasn't alone? 'Where are – um – Neil and his girlfriend?' she added cautiously.

'Fiancée. Have you forgotten the big announcement already? They wanted to get off early so they could tell her folks. They didn't want me to wake you.'

'What about Gail?' Tim frowned. Had she got the name wrong?

'It's ten o'clock. She's at school.'

'Ten!' she shrieked. She was always at her desk by eight. 'I must call Howard.' She leaped up, searching for her mobile phone, lifting knickknacks and other artefacts around what must have been the most hideous bedroom she had ever seen. The furniture was a flat-pack build-it-yourself job and to top it all, on the dressing-table sat a teddy bear clutching a crimson satin heart between its paws with the words 'I love you' embroidered on it. Suddenly enraged, she grabbed it, intending to sling it across the room. Instead, she pressed the soft white fur to her cheek and held it there.

'Who the hell's Howard?' said Tim, hopping from one suede shoe to the other as he tied the laces. Was she married to a man who wore suede shoes?

She sank back on the bed, still cuddling the bear, her mind a swampy mass of mud. She thought quickly. 'A new hairdresser.'

'Hairdresser? You? You hate hairdressers.'

'Someone told me he was very good.'

'Who?'

'Rita.' The name came from nowhere. Fortunately it satisfied Tim. He pecked her on the cheek and left.

Time to think hard. She tossed the bear aside.

Going over the events of the night before, what amazed her was how she managed to get through it without any of the strangers around her batting an eyelid. In this mad world, she was Tim's wife and Neil, a shambling scarecrow who towered above her was her son. Sulky Gail was her daughter. Luckily, she wasn't supposed to know anything about Helen, so she was able to direct most of her questions to her, even if it did make her sound like the future mother-in-law from Hell.

But what had put the tin lid on it was not so much theirs, but her own unfathomable acceptance of the situation. Not only that, it had been fun, in an unsophisticated sort of way, like playing Trivial Pursuit with a group of friends and a large bottle of wine. She hadn't laughed so much in years. There'd been a series of humorous toasts. 'To Gail's sweet smile!' 'To Dad and his vile taste in music.'

'Phil Collins, I ask you,' Neil had explained to Helen. That was it, she thought. That tape in the car. 'Easy Lover.' Tim was always singing it. One day she'd threatened to throw the tape in the river, but hadn't.

Tim had remained unabashed. 'It's better than your Mum's taste. I wish I'd never taken her to see Pavarotti. You know that night when it pissed down all night and we all caught colds. She was happy with Tom Jones before that. Now she thinks she's an opera buff.' And everyone had looked at her and laughed. But it wasn't unpleasant. It was like being attacked by a soft pillow.

At one point over pudding; Peach Pavlova, apparently one of her specialities, the scarecrow with the big smile, sorry, Neil, started reminiscing about a holiday cottage on the Suffolk coast they used to rent every August. 'Remember that crab I caught in a bucket and you found it in the kitchen next morning when you got up to cook breakfast and you screamed so loud, the neighbours called the police because they thought someone was being murdered?'

And the odd thing was she did remember. Clearly. She could see those bead-like black eyes peering out from under the sink. And she remembered Tim pouring her a tumblerful of brandy.

'And it wasn't even nine-o'clock in the morning!' she exclaimed to the assembled company and she knew she always said this whenever the story was repeated and everyone always laughed. Not at her. With her. With shared remembrance. It was like nothing she had ever experienced and had sunk gratefully into this strange soft quilt called family. She could see how too much of it could be suffocating, but there was enough air to keep her sharp.

Some of that feeling still lingered annoyingly as she concentrated on re-establishing her true identity. She hated quilts, cushions and other fripperies. Her flat was a lofty expanse of hardwood and paint. She recited a verbal CV. My name is Morag Melville. I am forty three years old. After graduating from Reading University with first class honours in Estate Management, I began work for a major agricultural insurance company, leaving that after ten years to set up my own consultancy advising on forestry investment. It's a specialist field and I've built up a good business. I employ Howard as my deputy and a PA called Shirley. I have never married. Never felt the need. I'm happy in my own company. I live in a deluxe riverside apartment in Maidenhead and I lead a fulfilling, busy life. I attend concerts, operas and read good literature. I have two Siamese cats called Solveig and Pier Gynt.

Something brushed past her legs. She picked it up. It was that fat scruffy tabby, Pussikins. She fondled its ear. It was torn and misshapen, but completely healed after his brush with next door's greyhound… She stopped. How the hell did she know that? Things were getting worse. She pushed the creature from her lap. It strutted from the bedroom its tail a vertical token of dented pride.

She dialled the office number. 'Melville Consultancy.' It was Howard.

'I'm running a bit late,' she said. 'I'll be with you in about half an hour.'

Howard sounded puzzled. 'Who are you?'

'It's me, you idiot. Morag.'

'Morag who?'

'Cut it out, Howard. April Fool's Day's been and gone.'

'If you give me your surname I'll check our records.'

She decided to play along. 'Put me through to your boss immediately.'

'I'm afraid Mr Melville is in a meeting. Can I take a message? Miss er…'

She slammed the phone down. If he was expecting a bonus this year, he'd have to think again. Mister Melville! Howard hadn't even the gumption to think up a different name.

The first thing to do was return to her flat and change. She always worked more efficiently in tailored clothes. What she found herself in now was reserved for lounging about at home. She telephoned for a taxi and hoped she had enough change in her raincoat pocket to pay the fare.

Her key that let her into the building jammed in the front door lock. It wouldn't turn however much she tried. As she struggled, she spotted the woman who lived in the next-door flat approaching. She didn't know her name. They kept themselves to themselves in Thameside Villas.

'There's something wrong with my key. It's a good thing you came along when you did or I'd be locked out.' She affected a stiff laugh and was reminded of the hilarity of the previous night. The scent of loss drifted by and was gone.

The woman gave her that look of a headmistress watching a cockroach scuttle across the Axminster. 'Do I know you?'

'Yes, you bloody well do,' Morag shouted back as the woman took her own keys out of her bag, let herself in the front door and slammed it shut in her face.

Get a grip, Morag, she told herself. Think again. The cleaner. Of course. She employed one through an agency. Her hours were nine to twelve. She'd be inside now.

She pressed the intercom.

Later she found herself wandering along the river. Yesterday's rain had cleared and the blue sheen of the sky was reflected in the sleek launches bobbing on their ropes.

A coxless four slid through water like a knife through mercury, their shoulder muscles rippling, their faces grimacing with the effort. By now it was lunch-time and shoppers and office workers alike were taking advantage of the early spring sunshine to eat outside. A fitful breeze teased the flags on the opposite bank. Muted traffic crossed and re-crossed the stone bridge.

It wasn't her fault she mistook the girl who answered the intercom for the cleaner. Her estuary English was as broad as Southend beach at low-tide. It turned out that not only was she a famous model but she insisted it was her flat, that she'd lived in it for two years and if she didn't leave her alone she'd call the law.

'If anyone calls the police, it will be me,' Morag had snapped back. 'You're squatting.'

'And you're mad, that's what you are. You want fucking certifying.'

'Well really!'

She hadn't called the police. She knew she'd have trouble making them understand. She had no proof of identity whatsoever. She thrust her fists into the pockets of the raincoat she was beginning to loathe with a murderous hatred and marched on. What a scruff she looked. What if she met someone she knew?

'Mo! What are you doing here? You don't usually come into town on Fridays.'

It was that man again. The one called Tim – her husband. Sitting on a bench facing the river, stuffing a white roll into his face, scattering crumbs much to the pleasure of a group of noisy ducks, paddling around his suede shoes. This was the man who'd slept alongside her last night but had fortunately kept to his side of the bed, otherwise she shuddered to think what might have happened. He quickly finished his meal and made room for her on the bench.

She sat down, slowly warming to his friendly and non-judgemental expression. In fact, she realised, she had never been so pleased to see anyone in her life. He smelled of cheap aftershave and hard-boiled eggs. She took a deep breath. 'I just felt like getting out of the house,' she explained. Which was true.

Tim seemed to accept this. 'You're looking more like your old self,' he said. 'A bit more colour in your cheeks. I never thought you'd be worried about entertaining your future daughter-in-law. She's perfect for Neil, isn't she?'

'I agree,' she replied slipping her hand into his, enjoying its rough warmth. 'She was very nervous though, wasn't she?'

'Do you remember when I took you to meet my parents for the first time?'

'I was terrified,' she said suddenly seeing an oak-panelled dining room and a table set with a multitude of knives and forks she hadn't a clue which to use when.

'But they fell in love with you just like I had.'

The ducks had waddled back into the river. Two swans were cruising not far from the bank, trailing two perfect interlocked Vs behind them. 'Can you remember when we first met?' she said.

'Remember? How could I forget? There I was single-skulling under Caversham Bridge, not a care in the world…'

'In Reading?'

'No, Venice, Silly. Venice, Berkshire.'

She found herself replying, 'Silly yourself.' What sort of expression was that?

'And there you were above me leaning over the parapet, chucking books into the river. I thought you'd dropped them by accident and tried to fish them out for you…'

'And your boat capsized!'

‘And when I was suffering the first stages of pneumonia you told me you’d chucked them on purpose because you were “sick of bloody boring estate management”.’

‘Did I say that?’

‘The language was probably much worse, knowing you, but that was the general drift.’

‘All that pneumonia rubbish was to get me to your flat to seduce me!’

‘Seduce?’ he said as they began to walk back up the steps away from the riverbank. ‘You were a willing partner, I seem to recall.’

‘Oh yes? It seemed pretty much like a seduction to me. You filled me with wine and I told you how I was at a cross-roads with my life and needed advice.’

‘And I said if you carried on with estate management you’d turn into a boring old maid stuck in one of those hideous luxury flats they were putting up along the river, with only two snooty Siamese cats for company.’

She shuddered. ‘Cold?’ he said with renewed concern. ‘Tell you what. Let’s go home. Gail’s staying at Avril’s overnight, isn’t she? So it’ll be just us. I fancy seducing you all over again.’

‘How about the other way round?’

‘We’ll do it whichever way round you like.’ She punched him playfully on the arm. He kissed her.

In the short walk to the car-park, everything fell into place. She had given up estate management and moved into Tim’s Reading flat next door to Huntley and Palmer’s factory where she worked boxing cream crackers. When Tim graduated he took a job in a bookstore and they married. Later he was promoted to be the manager of the Maidenhead branch. They left Reading and bought an affordable semi in a tree-lined avenue. They didn’t have any pets because Neil was allergic to them. Pussikins only came along after he’d left home. Gail was a surprise. Now aged fourteen with a strange taste in footwear they couldn't imagine being without her. Mo tucked her arm into his as they strolled past the Indian supermarket just before the car-park.

'Shall I buy a bottle of cheap plonk to remind us of old times?' she said suddenly.

'Good idea. I'll get the car and meet you outside.'

She pushed open the door and was immediately assailed by the mingled aroma of cardamom, turmeric and cinnamon. From somewhere, eastern music jangled, overlaid with commentary from a live cricket match. At first she found the smell exhilarating and breathed deeply. After a while it began to make her feel sick.

Her footsteps took her further into the depths of the shop to where a rough painted sign swinging from the ceiling proclaimed 'Fine Wines for the Disserning Shopper', in black felt-tip. She winced at the spelling error. Her eyes briefly ran along the shelves. Lambrusco, Soave, Chianti. What rubbish was this?

She marched up to the shopkeeper just as the commentator screamed, 'He's out! Caught in the slips for a duck.'

'Where are your vintage wines?' she demanded.

'Wine there,' he pointed. 'Very good.' He pressed his ear to the radio on the shelf-behind him from where the cricket commentary still trickled on.

She looked around her. What on earth was she doing here? She always ordered her wine from a highly reputable company in Windsor who delivered it promptly.

She left the shop. Her head buzzed as if it were tuned into a distant radio station. She felt weak and ever so slightly sick. She'd been working too hard. That was the trouble. She dashed across the road toward Thameside Villas. Just then a car emerged at a reckless speed from a nearby car park and almost ran her over. She stepped back quickly and scowled at the driver – a scruffy individual with hair the colour of rope. The car careened around the corner and was gone.

She had forgotten about the incident by the time she was slipping her key into the lock. She took a shower, fed the cats a slice of poached salmon each, opened the bottle of 1982 Bordeaux red and after slipping *Don Carlos* into the CD player sank into her leather sofa.

Outside dusk was painting the river with grey shadows and one by one the lights strung along the river bank came alight, throwing out bright streamers across the water. A rippling skein of geese flew overhead, their wings stained pink by the setting sun. This was her favourite time of the day; a moment for reflection. It had been another profitable day. She had acquired two new clients. Her accountant had agreed her tax-projections for the next financial year. 'Here's to me,' she said aloud, raising her glass to Pier Gynt and Solveig who, arranged tastefully on the windowsill, remained indifferent to her triumph.

And for reasons she couldn't begin to fathom, a single tear as round and perfect as a pearl rolled down her nose, and splashed into the blood-red wine.

THE WRECK OF THE VICTORIA ANNE

The moon's silver path beckons me across the water but I am not so addled by misery that I wish to follow it nor am I so short of wit not to know that, were I to do so, I would sink beneath the ocean and there join my John in his cold, watery grave. Besides, the moon will soon be gone, swallowed by the rising sun and another day will roll in with the rising tide, whether I wish it or not.

A ragged skein of geese cross the lightening sky, gossiping like Whitby fishwives, their wing tips snatching the first bite of the rising sun.

The man is here again, too, hugging the shadows. He watches and he waits as I watch and wait. But when I rise to leave, he will be gone as he has done for the past week. Time means nothing to me now. All I can think of is my old life before it was wrecked.

John and I locked our cottage door and gave the key to Minister Sheldon. He then helped us up into his carriage for the journey across the moor. He had raised the money for our passage on the *Victoria Anne* bound for Canada. I should write to him to say that his good wishes have come to naught and his money wasted. But I have neither the wit nor the want to do anything now. A new world goes on around me now. I do not belong to it. All I do now is rise betimes and sit on the far rim of the ocean and wait for the day to begin and when it does I go back to my lodging and wait for night to fall.

Mr Sheldon stopped the carriage when we came in sight of the sea. Although not thirty miles from where I had spent my two and twenty years, I had never seen it. It gleamed softly blue like Mrs Winthrop's best sateen sheets beneath my flat-iron. The wind sang gently and sweetly. The scent of heather, the murmuring diligence of the bees filled our hearts. He led us in prayer and we added our amens.

'The *Victoria Anne*,' he said when we had reached the wharf at Whitby and gazed upon the vessel sitting proud as a nesting swan in its berth.

'We are most obliged,' said John stepping back to avoid the throng of people pushing past us. There were more carts, carriages and wagons clattering across the cobbles than I had ever seen in one place. It struck me then that there would have been plenty of work for us in such a bustling place so close to where we were born and I nearly said to Mr Sheldon that we would try our luck there.

But I dared not. He had been so good to us. His eyes were fixed on the horizon that drew us towards a new life. Maybe he yearned for a new start himself, sick to death of his moorland parish and his flock of desperate faces, hungry eyes and broken spirits. But duty kept him bound there so he laid his dreams on our shoulders and sent us forth to a new land weighed down with his burden.

I could see that my husband had filled his basket brimful with the minister's dream. He gazed on the ship's bulk in awe. 'And a grand name, too,' he said, taking my hand but avoiding my eye lest my apprehension should find a home in his. 'It bears your name, my love. It is a portent that our luck is about to change.'

A curse more like.

Was it my fault then that our married life started with misfortune and never recovered: indeed dipped further? Was his death because he married his Victoria Anne? We had not been wed a week when John shattered his leg. A prop collapsed in Sheriff's Pit. It did not heal straight and then fever set in, after which he hadn't the strength to dig or load the railway wagons with ironstone and send them on their way clanging and screeching down to the furnaces in Middleborough.

People were good to us. Mrs Winthrop, for whom I still

worked, bought me six fat Swaledales from Malton Market, even though we did not worship at her church. She also fetched us a loom and I remember how proud John was when he sold our first length of fine wool in Kirkby Market.

Our first and our last.

The winter was wet and raw when our flock caught the black tongue and perished, one by one, as did my benefactress herself of the coughing disease the following spring. Her daughter-in-law then brought her own maid with her from Guisborough who had learned fancy ways in Newcastle. I was no longer needed.

'Indeed, God smiles on you,' said Mr Sheldon, brushing off talk of luck and portents like dust from his collar. But I ask myself. Does the Lord not punish us for turning our back on the church and following, instead, the teaching of John Wesley? The church was dedicated to St Lawrence and it is the Saint Lawrence River on whose black depths I now gaze that swallowed John so very near our journey's end? Did my husband smile because we so nearly – oh so nearly – reached land that we could taste its sweetness in the air and smell the grass of that vast new land awaiting us.

Every day, I sit here to wait for the dawn on the edge of a creek that turns its back on the open river, the haunt of the lost and discarded, where the washed-up flotsam of the tide slaps against the rotten piers. I savour the sun's rising because it makes sense to me. Sunrise is the same everywhere; the demons of strange darkness falling back and reshaping into familiarity.

We were not headed for this city of Quebec. We were only to disembark briefly here to a wait another vessel to carry us farther upstream where we had letters of introduction for a dissenters' community of farmers and loggers. It wasn't that I hadn't expected to feel strange at the beginning of our new life in the New World. We had talked about it, John and I, as we walked the stone track above the cottage we rented from the Winthrops but we had always thought we would have each other and our fellows in God to help guide us through the strangeness towards the light.

Now I am cut adrift, the thread is broken. The river is wider than any I have ever seen and the moon above it is a big as a cartwheel spilling its path of silver medallions. If I did ever reach the moon and walk across its mountains it would feel no less alien than what surrounds me now.

The man has stepped out of the shadows and leans against a fence, his face splashed with the dawn's light. He smokes a cigar as if it were a religion. I will stay my departure until he goes. But it would seem that he wishes to speak to me. I do not wish it. I turn from him and watch the stain of night above the deep river being rinsed clean by the eastern sky. Will my heart ever be rid of its stain of loss however hard the rubbing?

One of the *Victoria Anne*'s boilers exploded. We were all crowded on one side of the deck as the land rose towards us. Sheets of fire rose and showered the water. I was lucky, they said. A bulwark shielded me from the full force of the blast. God was smiling on me, they said. I was flung clear of the carnage and then hauled from the river, water streaming from my sodden skirts and hair. I was taken I know not where, sobbing for John and all I knew. The people who care for me say I am lucky but despise me because I have failed to acknowledge my good fortune. They would send me into the wilderness alone if they knew how much I would curse God had I the strength or will to do so.

Once I was dried, rested and fed, I was taken to make a deposition to the authorities and then to a lodging house where I was told my rent would be paid for two weeks. I now have one day left to me with no thought in my head of where to go or what to do after that. John was my anchor, my loom, my stave. The warp and weft of existence has unravelled for me. I am deaf to its rhythms. They dance to a different melody here from the one I once knew.

The man approaches me at last. Had I been sitting with my spinning-wheel outside my cottage in Rosedale I would have bade him good day and no more. I knew who I was there and my place in it. Here I am as blank as the night sky, as a book with no words printed within its pages. Yet there is something about his bearing that reminds me of John when he asked me to walk home with him from haymaking; the bold, yet shy, stance of a young stag, the eye wary, the sudden backwards leap at the snap of a twig. But as he nears I see he is nothing like John. He is taller but narrower in the shoulder. He stops in front of me and removes his hat.

'Ma'am?' He is an English-speaker; no trace of the French gabble that surrounds me here although his way of talking is still strange to me. He offers me a cigarette from a silver case although he still holds his cigar between his thumb and forefinger. This is a land of fancy cigarettes in silver cases, of vast skies and expectations. Perhaps there are cigarettes in York or London or other cities that I have never seen but they were unknown in our dale. The only man I ever saw smoke a cigarette before was a pedlar who arrived one day with a scarlet cloth about his neck, leading a dappled horse got up in ribbons which he sold for a penny each. We chased him from our midst when chickens began to go missing from the coops and Mrs Sheldon lost a pie from her larder and my mistress a ring from her dressing-table.

But we suspected him before that. He did not belong to

us as I do not belong to this place where people smoke cigarettes from silver cases. This is a new land where the emptiness I wear like a scarlet cloth about my neck is not welcome. They do not like people who sit and mourn. This is a land of doing and getting.

God helps those who help themselves, they say. So I no longer care for God. And yet I live. The sun rises and the sun sets and I am here and John is gone.

The man cocks his head towards the tethered boat in the shimmering moonlight's path heaped with wreaths that marks the place where the *Victoria Anne* foundered. 'You were on it.'

It is not a question. He hands me his card. So he's a newspaper man. But that's not what catches my eye. It is the name. Anthony Peirson. Its spelling: the 'e' before the 'I'.

I grasp a tenuous thread that links my life now to my life before, tie it to my heart. 'There are Peirsons where I come from. Many more lie in the graveyard.'

I look at him more closely and see nothing else that reminds me of what I have left behind; only his sun-cracked face, his clear eyes, his embroidered waistcoat, his shiny shoes and his city suit with its velvet buttons.

'My father was a Rosedale man, an iron miner, until an accident prevented him from working underground. He made his way here fifty years before.'

'It was the same for my John,' I say.

Together we follow another slack rope of geese squabbling overhead until they are pulled over the horizon into the golden arc of the sun.

'I read your deposition,' he said. 'It was very brief and said little. If you tell me the full story I will pay you handsomely.'

'I don't want your money,' I say. 'I would not wish to profit from my husband's death.'

He flings the spent butt of his cigar into a corner of oily water where it bobs like a cork in the scum.

'Fair enough,' he says. 'They serve a fine breakfast at Duckett's. As much as you can eat for a dollar. That's where I'm bound.'

'That would be fine if I had a dollar to my name,' I say, testing the unfamiliar word beneath my tongue.

He thrusts his hands in his pockets and begins to walk away. 'I have two dollars and plenty more where that came from,' he calls over his shoulder.

His steps are long and the gap between us widens. He is something I do not know and yet he has our dale within him. Nothing remains of John, where we came from and what we came for. Gone like the moon, outshone by the sun climbing strongly above the river. The rules have been rewritten, the loom rethreaded, the rhythms re-set. What have I to lose when I have lost everything that was of me and is me?

I stand up and hasten after him. I quicken my English steps to match his New World strides. Then and now. Warp and weft. Two singular threads making one cloth.

THE ZANCANI CELLO

We found the cello by chance. We were on our honeymoon in Budapest where we had rented a room in a clean but shabby hotel. And there it was, wrapped in old newspaper under the bed. The owner shrugged and said it had been left behind by a Spanish lady and that it was probably as riddled with woodworm as she had been with consumption.

Despite an accumulation of grime it filled the bedroom with a golden glow. The wood was of the finest satinwood and the back was painted with the image of a saint or angel. I wondered whether it was a Stradivari or an Amati and decided to consult scholars and musicians.

'Just think of the money we could make,' I said.

Sarah glared. 'I don't care if it's worthless. It's mine and it's never leaving my side.'

From that moment on she never allowed me to touch it – or her. She caressed its curves and belly as if it were her lover and together they made the sweetest and saddest music.

Whoever I asked told me I should show it to Professor Williams of the Royal Academy of Music.

That night Sarah locked me out of the bedroom and I knew I had been usurped by a greater love.

After an exchange of letters, Professor Williams and I finally met in his Oxford lodgings. Over port, he leaned forward in his chair. 'My wife and I spent our honeymoon in Venice. Jane was a cellist of some distinction Ever since we met I had been seeking an instrument to match her talent and beauty. It was *Carnivale* but we avoided the noisy crowds and wandered through the quiet alleys, arm in arm. Then a sea-fret drifted in from the lagoon, shrouding the buildings and muffling all sounds but the slap of green water against the walls.' He paused and looked far beyond the panelled wood and his untouched glass. I think he had forgotten I was there.

'The mist lifted for a moment,' he eventually continued, 'to reveal a dingy shop. In the window stood a cello; a cello so exquisite that we knew it was waiting for us. The *padrone* seemed only too eager to part with it.

'We were so excited with our find we decided to return home immediately. You see, we both knew what it was.' He looked at me. 'What do you know of Isepo Zancani?'

Before I could answer, he stood up and ushered me to the door.

My continued research led me to the Edinburgh's University Library. It was only when I opened the first book on the pile at my desk, I realised I had not asked the professor what happened once they owned the cello.

I found very little to begin with. Signor Zancani is a mystery. Some say he never existed; others that he lived in Cremona but disappeared, died or was incarcerated in an asylum, after having made only one instrument.

One book contained a paragraph more from the realms of fairy-tale than history. The story was that Zancani was apprenticed to the celebrated Nicolò Amati with whom Antonio Stradivari also learned his trade.

One day, a Lombardy financier and his daughter called on the great Amati. She was a gifted cellist and he wanted to buy her best instrument money could buy. Because he was mean and, knowing the prices Signor Amati charged, he suggested his apprentices each make one and he would buy the one that pleased him best. They all set to work, none more assiduously that Isepo Zancani for, you see, had fallen in love with the beautiful girl. He worked all day and all night for months. And win the contest he did, with the most exquisite instrument on which he himself painted the portrait of the Virgin fashioned in the image of the beautiful flaxen-haired Francesca. The financier was delighted. Then Zancani fell to his knees and asked for his daughter's hand in marriage. Even worse than the 'No!' shouted by the man, Francesca began to laugh and couldn't stop because not only was Zancani a poor apprentice, he was short and had a face like an artichoke.

Isepo pointed at her and prophesied she would be the last woman to mock him. He said that any woman who touched that cello would fall in love with it and be his until death and beyond. Still the girl laughed. Zancani fled and was never seen again.

Within a week, Francesca was dead. She had been playing the cello when a string broke and struck her across the face. The wound became septic. On the day of her funeral, her father hurled the cello in the river.

I wrote again to the professor about the story I had uncovered and to ask him what happened to his wife. He refused to see me but sent me this reply. 'Jane died within a month of our honeymoon. The cello killed her. I went to her room to destroy it but it had vanished. Now do you see?'

It was at that moment that madness seized me too. I had to destroy the cursed instrument. I gave Sarah a strong sleeping draft and stole it from her.

I sat on a bench by the river. Rain spattered my face but I felt nothing but hot rage. I opened the case. I carefully unwound the silk cloth Sarah had wrapped around her 'beauty'.

The case was empty.

She had tricked me. I was too late. When I returned home I found her on the bedroom floor, as cold and unyielding as the cello in her arms.

When I returned with the doctor, my Sarah was still dead but the cello had gone.

That was fifty years ago. I am now old and weary and close to death. I still search for news of the Zancani Cello.

WHITE MAN VAN

November. Cath sips her coffee and shivers. Her bungalow stands on the shore road facing the grey North Sea. The nearest other permanent resident is a man of her own age whose bungalow stands half a mile or so up the road. An ex-banker, someone said. In the summer, he takes his boat out. She doesn't know what he does the rest of the year. She isn't interested. It isn't that sort of place. She isn't that sort of person.

Cath sloshes Bushmills into her coffee. She pulls a thick document out of a jiffy bag and thumps it down in front of her old Imperial. She is running out of ribbons and the 'h' key sticks but it suits her. Besides, the electricity is unreliable here. She hasn't a landline telephone and mobile reception is patchy. That's fine by her, as well. She's not a people person.

She works all morning, blowing on her fingers. The keys peck the paper, the wind howls, the waves roar and seagulls fight on her roof. In the afternoon she drives twenty miles to the nearest village and stocks up with jars of coffee, tins of this and that, cartons of long-life milk, and oranges. She can't find any Irish whiskey at the Cash and Carry. She has to make do with Bells. Her rusty old Datsun is a petroholic, so she usually makes a detour to the cheapest garage. Only today it's closed.

Not a good day she thinks as she drives home. The wind is getting up. Fat clouds lumber across the sea. As she passes the ex-banker's bungalow, she sees another vehicle parked next to his beaten-up Land-Rover. A white van.

As she chugs by, a shock of blonde hair and a pair of long blue legs emerge from underneath the van. Eyes meet. She doesn't see the fuel gauge needle slump like a drowning man's arm.

Two minutes later, the inevitable happens. Fighting the wind, she begins the trudge back to ex-banker's bungalow. The door is opened by the vision of blonde hair and long blue legs. The middle-aged man is nowhere to be seen. Cath explains her predicament. 'No probs,' he says. 'The old man's got plenty of cans in the shed.' He disappears. His voice calls back, 'You've not got a cat, I take it?'

'Cat?' she jumps. 'No. Nor a dog,' she stammers. 'I live alone.'

He returns with a can and a grin. 'Cat – Catalytic converter. Unleaded. If you're green, you're knackered. The old fart's only got four star.'

'That's – that's fine.' Bugger. Here she is, the wrong side of forty and she's behaving like an adolescent, or worse – a mad menopausal woman. He flicks blonde hair from his eyes and her stomach melts. He's bloody gorgeous. His skin is a fine suede she aches to stroke.

When she gets home, she slings her shopping across the floor, knocks back a tumbler full of neat Bell's. How long is it since she'd had sex? Too bloody long.

It's one of those days when the air's so cold you can chip the edges off the sky with a spade. Time for another coffee. A knock at the door. Bloody Gorgeous is standing there, looking, well, bloody gorgeous.

'So,' he says. 'Aren't you going to invite me in?'

Cath feels a rush of blood and it isn't to her head. 'Are you making a pass?' she says. God, she's rusty. Her sexuality creaks like old bed springs. What if he's only come to borrow a cup of sugar? He'll think she's an old tart.

'I'm not passing. I'm staying.'

November becomes December. Gulls screech mournfully. Rain hammers splinters of ice into the roof. Fog rolls across the road. His name is Greg, is as spectacular out of clothing and under sheets as one might expect. He makes the occasional foray into the outside world for food and cigarettes (nobody's perfect) but otherwise they live in steamy solitude.

'Haven't you got a job or anything?' Cath asks him one day as he slowly runs his tongue along her spine.

'Nope.'

'Well I have.'

'Oh yeah. Translator of German scientific journals. What sort of a job is that?

'Least I've got a job…'

'And what sort of life? Alone, knocking back Irish whiskey and that disgusting coffee that tastes like boiled rucksacks, dressed like a raggle-taggle-gypsy-O. When you're dressed that is.'

'So why are you here?'

'Something to do.'

She throws a pillow, but before she scores a hit, he has rolled on top of her and smothered her with his mouth, his hand cupping the soft middle-aged sag of her breast.

Outside the fog persists. She likes fog. It smothers the hard edges.

Later, Greg finds an old radio under the bed. 'Any batteries in this?' He shakes it. It crackles into life. 'Attention all shipping. The Meteorological Office issued the following gale warning to shipping at 0600 hours GMT, today, December 25th. Humber. Northerly. Severe gale force 9 imminent…'

Christmas Day. A time for families, people.

Someone is hammering on the door.

'Carol singers,' she laughs but feels a shiver of reality down her spine. She flings a sheet around her and opens the door. It catches the wind and flies out of her hand. The full force of an easterly gale hits.

It's Greg's father. He pushes past her with a growl. 'Have you a telephone?'

Greg is behind her fully dressed. How did he do that? 'What's up Dad? Come to rescue me from the clutches of The Older Woman?'

And suddenly Cath knows she's a toy, a diversion, a decoy in the complicated animosity between father and son.

'I'm over eighteen you know. Big boy.'

'Big fool. I don't give a toss what you do. I'm here to call the coastguard. Saw a boat go out a while back. Now it's upside down.'

'Haven't you got a phone?' asks Cath.

Greg's father throws her a look of such utter contempt, she shrinks. 'Of course I've got a phone. But I thought I'd have a bit of fun, tramp along in a force ten gale, get frozen stiff and waste valuable time when someone could be drowning out there. Of course I haven't got a bloody phone!

Cath hasn't got one either. At least, not one that gets a signal here.

'The pub!' Greg cries. What pub? She didn't know there was a pub. 'They've got a phone.' Greg grabs his father's arm and they're gone. Together.

She sees the crumpled bed, the overflowing ash-tray, clothes strewn across the floor, the empty bottles, the dirty plates. She is engulfed by a tidal wave of loneliness.

It's one of those rare January days, when the sky is blue pearl. A deceitful day that reminds you of lilacs and daffodils, before blasting you with another cannonade of winter. A mocking day that looks young but makes you feel as old as the ocean. Early that morning, a man digging for worms found a bloated body washed up against a break-water ten miles further down the coast. It's time she moved. Time she lived.

HOOKERS GREEN

When we arrived at the *Loch View* guesthouse, the sky darkened.

Mum said, 'It looks like rain.'

Dad squeezed her hand. 'This is Scotland, remember. You weren't hoping for a tan, were you?'

They exchanged fond smiles and I knew all was fine with my eleven-year-old world. The family holiday was something we always looked forward to. Mum painted her watercolours. Dad was a photographer for the local rag and enjoyed the freedom wild-life photography gave him. I was to be responsible for the holiday journal. I would keep a diary and copy out extracts from guidebooks, paste in tickets, dried flowers, seaweed – that sort of thing. Only I didn't, not after…

The owner introduced herself as Moira Mackenzie and said she ran the place with her husband, Jim, although we never saw him.

'That Moira is a stunner, isn't she?' Dad said when we were settling into our room overlooking the loch. 'What colour would you call her eyes, Helen?'

'Hookers Green?' Mum ventured.

'Miaow,' he said, kissing her nose.

She adopted an air of innocence. 'What? It's a perfectly proper paint colour, as well you know.'

'I believe you,' Dad said, holding is hands up. He then picked up his camera from the bed. 'I'm off out. The light on the water just now is amazing.' He was right. The surface of the loch gleamed like softly-buffed pewter over which the shadow of the forest cast a mossy sheen. 'Coming?'

I nodded but Mum said, 'I'm a bit tired.' She'd not fully recovered from a bout of flu in the spring.

We met Moira again in the hall. She and Dad started

talking, ending up discussing the fabled monster. As they talked, I watched her. She *was* beautiful but it was a cold beauty and I didn't like it. Her hair was black, her skin pale and her green eyes glittered with amusement as she told us about a previous guest. 'He was a wee fellow with a pointed beard. He was absolutely certain of its existence and that it belonged to a race of giant lizards that rule the universe. How crazy can you get?' She laughed and then opened a drawer in the hall table. 'Here! Have one of these. Compliments of the House.' She threw something and Dad caught it.

It was one of those mascots people hang from their car mirrors. It was made of soft green, trembling plastic with a garish tartan beret glued to its head. But what frightened me were its over-sized googly eyes.

Dad recoiled in mock horror. 'Good Lord; that is *hideous*!'

Was it only me that saw that venomous flash in Moira's eye? I blinked and it was gone.

'Och, now you've hurt Wee Nessie's feelings,' she joked.

'I'd better make amends by fixing it in the car straight away,' said Dad, still chuckling as we went out.

At breakfast the next day, Mum peered over her coffee cup at the rain sheeting across the water. She said she wasn't hungry but Dad and I tucked into Moira's full Scottish breakfast.

Tangled clouds hung over the dark water, their hems trailing unevenly as if they'd come unstitched. There was nothing else to do but go for a drive. It was a dreary outing; mile after mile of dark water, grey trees, grey hills – and rain sluicing down the windows. All the while, Wee Nessie wobbled and goggled as if it knew something we didn't. I wanted to throw it away but Dad said it cheered him up. Mum seemed untroubled.

Only, the following morning, she said she didn't want to go down for breakfast. Dad promised to bring her up a pot of coffee. I was listless. I still hadn't got anything to put in my journal apart from the receipt from lunch the day before in a dismal café where we'd been the only customers. Dad, at least, hadn't lost his appetite and while he munched his toast, he chatted to Moira who seemed to have nothing else to do. 'Would you mind if I took some photographs of you?' he said.

'Me? Why?' She lifted her chin and widened her glassy eyes.

'Because you're beautiful,' Dad said, in a low voice that was somehow not his own.

I stood up, knocking the spoon out of my empty porridge bowl. It clattered to the floor. '*I'll* take Mum her coffee.' Dad had forgotten.

The rain didn't let up that day or the next. Mum stayed in the bedroom with a sketchbook open on her lap, staring at the loch, her pencil immobile in her hand, the paper bare.

Once again, Dad set up his tripod in Moira's private sitting-room. I watched for a while. Neither paid me any attention. Dad snapped away, sounding like one of those prancing fashion-photographers he so despised. 'Turn your head… look at the camera… lovely… make love to it… that's it… perfect…'

They didn't see me slip away.

And so it went on until the morning of the day we were due to leave. Something felt strange when I woke up. The curtains were open and the rain had stopped. The double-bed was empty. I quickly dressed and ran down to the dining-room. Moira was standing alone by the window, staring at the loch.

'Where are they?'

'Who, dear?' she said, without turning.

'Mum and Dad!' Was I screaming? I can't remember.

'Oh, *them*?' She shrugged.

I stumbled outside and bumped into Dad on his way back in, his camera slung round his neck. He was whistling. 'I saw an osprey catch a fish. Got a great shot.'

'Where's Mum?'

'Isn't she…?

'No.'

He ran towards the loch. He was gone for ages but came back shaking his head. He called the police.

They found her body at dusk, caught in a clump of submerged roots further downstream. There were stones in her pockets.

Green stones.

'Hookers Green,' Dad said. And then he wept.

POSTCARDS FROM LILA

I'm taking liberties, I know, Dear, telephoning you at your office. Only, I'm bored. Why? Because I'm having to sit here resting my poor, swollen ankles, watching the what I think is the sea recede to infinity. I should be well into the latest adventures of Millie Wagstaff. But the silly girl has clammed up on me and ink dries up in my Parker for want of inspiration. I've even switched to a pencil but it's no use. It's too hot for baby, me, my pen or Millie Wagstaff. I could take a stroll along the pier seeking ideas. Doctor Williams said it would do me good but it's too hot, I'm as big as a whale – or an airship – and don't want to frighten the donkeys. You're laughing at me, Will Marchmont. I can hear it in your voice. But it's the dreaded Lila who's put me in mind of airships.

Yes, another postcard! That's at least one a day since Llangollen. Not content with disturbing my solitude among the mountains, desperately scribbling undisturbed to finish off *Millie Wagstaff and the Sinister Suffragette,* I live in fear that she'll seek me out here in Southend, too. So let's hope this heatwave continues. If it's too hot for her to move an inch, as she complains, so she'll hardly make it to Southend. Mind you, she'd find anywhere too hot for her this summer, given her size. I know, I know. Catty. Unworthy of the young wife of an up-and-coming merchant banker or even Pauline Marchmont, celebrated authoress of the Millie Wagstaff Mysteries.

Then again, I don't see why I have to be sympathetic to a woman who tells me she has a medical reason for her enormous bulk and then never stops eating. You wouldn't believe how many cream-cakes she demolished in Llangollen.

Sorry, I'm nattering on. I can see you sighing and

desperately pretending to be listening to one of your tedious banking associates in case Sir Frederick happens to pop in your office. Yes, I know I shouldn't telephone you at work, darling – I take it London is even hotter than here – but I have so very little to distract me in Southend. My only entertainment is the sight of my fellow guests setting off to the beach or the pier; the ladies twirling bright parasols and showing off their nineteen-inch waists; the men with boaters atop shiny red faces and peeling noses thinking they're the bee's knees rather than music-hall comics. Don't you just love the British on holiday? Only, where's the sea? It's called Southend-on-Sea, for heaven's sake but the tide goes out for miles and I can't be bothered to go and dip my boiling toes in it.

Crabby? Sorry, darling, but you'd be crabby, too, waiting for baby while he kicks all day and night trying to escape. Mind you, the sea-air must be doing me some good. I managed bacon and eggs this morning! (Don't worry, I'm not going to turn into Lila! I'm too vain.) But I'd rather be in beautiful Llangollen, with you, this time, and not a seaside guest-house trying desperately to keep out of everyone's way and their questions about baby and what names we've chosen and if we want a boy. It's hardly scintillating conversation. And I miss you, too, darling boy. You will be able to take some leave this year, won't you? I am desperate to exorcise the memories of that woman. I'm terrified she'll pop out from behind every ice-cream parlour or tea shop with her 'Coo-ee, dear!' and her 'Not 'arfs'.

Yes, I know she means well and there's no harm in her but I wish she hadn't made a beeline for me that first day in Wales. All I did was take pity on her and invite her to my breakfast table my very first day because the other ladies seemed not to want to talk to her. I now know why, of course, but the damage is done. She wouldn't leave me alone after that. I feel I'll be stuck with her forever and her postcards.

Yes, I said. *Another* postcard. Not just two. You're not listening, darling. She sends one every day. Six, so far. And she will keep calling me Poppy. I was foolish enough to blurt out your pet name for me but made it clear she should call me Pauline. But would she take the hint? She never listens to anyone else but herself.

According to her latest missive – if I can make any sense of it at all – someone called Percy is being impossible and hasn't telephoned. And that Agnes (wife, sister, mother – who cares? I'd lost interest and was thinking of Millie) was forever staring out of the window, and I quote – 'looking for airships I should think.' I expect this Agnes couldn't bear listening to Lila a moment longer than two minutes like everyone else. Even her sons have gone as far away from her as is humanly possible until they learn how to build sky-rockets. She says her 'big boy', David, who went to live in South Africa (or was it South America?) is the spit of you. Lord above! As if. She only saw you briefly when you came to collect me from Llangollen in the Wolseley. And the younger son, Jack, had gone to 'seek his fortune' in Canada where he married a Red Indian squaw! She's lost her appetite because of it – or so she says. The sale of cream cakes in Watford must have plummeted in that case. Have you read about it in The Times?

Don't you dare *miaow* me, Will Marchmont!

You're right. But there is something about that woman that gets under my skin. It's all my own fault – as ever. I shouldn't have given her this address, but at least once I go home, she won't know where I am, so I shall be free.

Yes, you're right again. (That's why I adore you, you know!) I shall miss her in a strange sort of way. I suppose it's because I have nothing else to distract me since Millie

SNAP DECISION

'Jesus, Mary, what's all this junk?'

Bridie Durcan emerged, rump first, from under my bed and brushed dust from her starched apron. 'No wonder you wheeze.'

'That junk, Mrs Durcan, is the story of my life. Destroy that and I might as well be dead.'

She wagged an accusatory finger. 'We'll not have that now I'm in charge.'

In charge? She'd only entered my life the day before. She was the compromise I'd accepted when I told them I wasn't going into a home. Me, one of the *enfants terribles* of the late twentieth century – in a *home*? Andy Warhol called me his mentor (mind you, he was pissed at the time) and David Bailey told *The Irish Times* I taught him everything he knew – and more.

And Bridie Durcan itched to throw it all away.

She returned later with a plateful of something suspiciously like dog food with a side-serving of shamrock, propped me up and spooned it into my mouth, wiping my dribbles with a napkin. Oh, how are the mighty fallen.

'So you took snaps, did you, before you took the cloth?' she said. 'Any good, were they?'

'Any good? I'll have you know I was brilliant. None of this digital stuff then, you know. It took skill, deadly poisons swilling about in trays and drying prints pegged across my dark room as stiff as nuns' knickers.'

'Is that so? A little less chatting and more eating, if you don't mind then you can have some afters. You won't have tasted anything like my rice pudding.'

'I don't doubt it,' I said. 'Will I need a knife and fork?'

'And less of your cheek.'

* * *

One thing I soon learned about Bridie Durcan was that she never gave up. She burst in the next day, armed to the teeth with brush, bucket, dustpan and a fistful of bin-bags. 'Let's blitz this germ factory right now.'

That was it. I swung my legs out of the bed but I hadn't reckoned on the lethal hospital corners she insisted on which welded my to the bed. They grabbed my legs as I launched a flying tackle against the offending weapons of mass destruction. 'Over my dead body!' I shouted.

My prophecy was almost fulfilled. I ended up on the floor, with my pyjama trousers round my ankles and one of my coughing fits.

We looked through my 'junk' after supper. Bridie was unimpressed. Not even by the series Yoko Ono had raved about in Time Magazine. She took no interest in the composition, the placing of shadow and light, the depth of field. A stunning monochrome of Marilyn Monroe elicited a pitying shake of her head and Woody Allen gazing towards Times Square. 'A sharp, odd little man.'

Given her limited artistic eye, it wasn't long before the only item left was an old biscuit tin. She spent so long prising off the rusted lid that I felt dying would have been the more exciting option.

Then. 'Jesus!' and a hundred unframed prints sprang free like Jack from a box and slid to the floor.

'Now these are much more interesting,' she said, stooping to pick them up. 'Is that your mother? Oh and this must be you – weren't you the darling boy in your little trousers and school cap?' On and on she went. I closed my eyes.

It was the silence that woke me. I looked at her. Her face was radiant and she was praying.

Between her trembling fingers she held a small black and white print. Did you take this?'

'You'll miss the last bus if you don't go now.'

'Well, did you?'

'Of course I bloody well took it.'

'Then, look at it, you silly man.'

I snatched it from her. My God.

I couldn't have been more than twenty. I was on my way home to my flat after a particularly wild party and was probably full of happy pills, magic mushrooms and a lot more besides. It was January, well after midnight, and a mist was rising from the Liffey and drifting through the narrow streets. Anyway, I was soon lost. I staggered about for hours, slowly sobering up and feeling like Hell.

It began to rain. I turned a corner and there he was. An old man staring into the window of a harp shop, of all places, as if selecting the model to take with him into the afterlife. He was stooped; snowy-haired and his eyes couldn't have been up to much by the way he was struggling to focus. What the hell was he doing out at that time of night?

My Leica was in my shoulder-bag. It was my talisman then, my fetish, my religion. I couldn't wait. I wanted that shot. I would have killed for that shot.

Nothing mattered but me and him. It was the first time I'd felt something beyond me, more important than me. He remained oblivious to me as I prowled around him, seeking the perfect shot.

I pressed the shutter once. When I looked up, he'd gone.

I developed that photograph the next day. I watched the man emerge again like a ghost from the blank paper and take shape and I knew it was the last photograph I would ever take. I put it away with all the others and never looked at any of them again – until now.

'Well?' said Bridie.

I didn't have to say anything. What wasn't clear then,

was now. The man in the photograph; the man my arrogant, selfish, pleasure-seeking self-had snapped, was me; me as I am now. White-haired, half-blind, arthritic. Dying.

Bridie turned her gaze from me to the crucifix above the bed. 'It was a sign.'

'Maybe.'

'There's no "maybe" about it, Father Kerrigan. Now how about a nice mug of cocoa before I tuck you in for the night?'

I nodded. 'Only, this time, spare me your hospital corners.'

BETWEEN THE FIRST AND SECOND STRIKE

The village of Cailloux-Sainte-Cecile pants like an old dog in the heat. The church clock strikes one. The cracked note hovers above the rooftops then dissolves. Thérèse appears at her door, as she does every day at this hour.

She lives alone at the very top of the village. From her house, a narrow street hobbles down past the village graveyard that jealously guards its dead and along the grey flanks of the church that again strikes the hour. It then turns left, squeezes between dusty shuttered cottages still bearing their bullet grazes. At the bottom of the hill it sinks into a rectangle of beaten earth. Later, here in the evening shade, old men will play pétanque and talk of old times.

Beyond, a field of maize rustles under a jet of water that wafts to and fro in lazy swathes. The maize is ripe. An army of starlings gorges on its plump kernels. Monsieur Tapis, who rents the fields from Monsieur le Maire, oils his gun and grunts into his moustache.

High above him Thérèse shakes crumbs from her tablecloth. Three hens scuttle out from the shade of an upturned wheelbarrow. She kicks them away, takes the cloth back in the kitchen and returns with a bentwood chair.

In an ivy-clad mansion at the foot of the hill lives old Natalie Bouchier. She lives alone, too, but today her great-grand-daughter, Brigitte has come to visit. They have been playing a long and laborious game of bezique. The old woman's head droops over her cards.

Brigitte is bored. She looks through the wide open doors of the drawing-room with its jumble of china figurines and photographs, through the high iron gates and the tumble of hot, scarlet geraniums in their baked-earth pots along the wall. The paint-box blue sky beckons. She shuffles. 'It isn't what you think,' the old widow murmurs before sinking into a deeper sleep.

Brigitte creeps through the doors, skittering the gravel on the terrace, and slips through the gates and into the street. Once away from the shadows of the black cypresses the heat is fierce. Like the street she meanders uphill to no obvious purpose.

Thérèse, too, has fallen asleep on her bentwood chair. She hears them coming. Tramp. Tramp. Tramp. Up the hill.

But the boots belong to a troop of Dutch back-packers. They consult their guide book which says there is a fine monument to the Maquis in the cemetery. They reach the gates. They rattle the catch. The keys are in Thérèse's pocket. But she sleeps on. The back-packers march back down the street and the air congeals behind them into hot stillness.

Thérèse saw them first. She could climb higher than any of the village boys and that day she was swinging her legs in an elbow of the oldest apple tree in the orchard. Her beloved brother, Thierry, ran the farm now her parents were dead. He was in the fields cutting maize. He was too frightened to tell her he was in love with Natalie. She and her widowed mother ran the café. She was the prettiest girl in the village and Thérèse thought the family beneath her and Natalie a fool.

The village was as still as stone. Nothing moved. Unseen, Thierry and his friends crept from the village and into the surrounding hills, leaving the women and the old men to face the enemy.

The occupiers were more an irritation than a threat. They were there. That was all. Most of them were billetted with Natalie and her mother. Was it only Thérèse who watched them bloom and fatten while the rest of the village grew lean?

Her contempt festered into an irrational hatred as she shouldered the burden of the farm. She wore her brother's clothes and stomped about in his boots with a defiance that suppressed ridicule. No-one, not even her neighbours, suspected it was she who passed news and supplies to her male contemporaries camped under the stars or how she yearned to join them and not have to stagnate with the likes of Natalie.

No-one could say that the farm flourished under the occupation, but no-one starved. Natalie came up the hill once to ask for food, but Thérèse sent her packing, the little slut. The Germans took all her produce anyway. She always spat in the cans before she handed the milk over; made sure the rats had got to the grain. Her muscles hardened, her breasts shrank to nothing, her hair was short, her face bronzed and lined. She chopped wood. She mended the roof when a hailstorm shattered some tiles. She harvested what little maize was left after the German soldiers had used the field for target practice. Sweat soaked her back but she was proud.

And even as she dreams, the starlings stab the plump kernels with their thieving beaks. But it is no longer her concern. Stiff joints and dwindling funds forced her to sell her land to the Mayor twenty years ago. Now he rents it out to old Monsieur Tapis, who is waiting for the harvester to come and curses the starlings.

Brigitte finds a stone as white and smooth as a sugared almond. She kicks it up the steep hill, past the church and cemetery. Then she kicks it too fiercely and loses it in a ditch. She searches for a while before losing interest. It is only a stone and Cailloux-Sainte Cecile is full of stones.

When she looks up she sees a wrinkled old woman

folded in sleep on a bentwood chair. Her hands flutter in agitation, although her eyes are firmly shut. She must be dreaming, thinks Brigitte. She can't imagine what an ugly old woman with wrinkles as deep as plough furrows has to dream about.

She has reached the top of the village. The road ends at the gates of the walled graveyard. Brigitte isn't interested in graveyards. In a field beside the old woman's house is a gnarled apple tree, propped up by a metal rod. She picks an apple, but it is small and sour. She tosses it to some scratching hens.

The church clock strikes. One. Two. Brigitte rubs her hands against the bark of the apple tree. It is old and gnarled. Everything in this village is old.

The church clock strikes again. One. Two. Why does it strike twice, she wonders. Which one is the right time, the first or the second strike? They can't both be right. Does time stand still between the two strikes? Such things worry her.

Yes, the old woman dreams, she ran that farm well. She could still have it now had that cow not gone into labour when it did. She had struggled with it for hour upon hour as day darkened to night. The beast was already exhausted by the time she found the birthing ropes.

To her annoyance and shame, she did not have the strength to use them. She ran down the hill and banged on doors but no-one wanted to help proud Thérèse. In the end she was forced to try the café.

Natalie opened the door. From behind her steamed a rich, fatty mixture of garlic and red meat, along with the sound of music and drunken German voices. Natalie looked flushed. They could have been friends had Thérèse known Natalie's love for Thierry and her contempt for the

Germans: had she known that she cried herself to sleep every night ashamed of the way her mother indulged her visitors. But Thérèse only saw a pretty girl in the house of the enemy.

'One of my cows is in trouble. I need help.'

'What do you want me to do?' said Natalie, glancing behind her. 'I know nothing about animals.'

'Do you think I don't know that? Find someone who does, idiot.'

'Who?' Laughter breaks out behind her. 'I must go.'

Thérèse thrusts a boot into the closing door. 'If that cow dies, so do you, Slut.'

Tears trembled on Natalie's eyelashes. 'I'll try.'

Thérèse grabbed her hair that slipped like silk in her fingers. 'You'd better. Slut.'

'It's not what you think.'

'How dare you presume to know what I think?'

Thérèse stomped back to the barn. From time to time the cow moaned. In the corner of the barn rats scuttled under the straw. Thérèse cursed Natalie and cursed herself for having to ask her.

It was almost dawn when she heard the barn door creak open. 'Where the hell have you been?' But it wasn't Natalie.

'I saw the light,' the soldier said in good French. 'Is there a problem?'

She hadn't seen him before. He was very young. His ears stuck out at right-angles from cruelly cropped hair.

'The calf's stuck. I think it's dead.' Thérèse cocked her head towards the cow, now lying on its side, breathing in shallow gasps.

'I can help, please?'

Thérèse snorted.

'I am a farmer's son. My name is Helmut.'

Thérèse couldn't imagine any farms in Germany. That country was one big factory with belching chimneys and red furnaces forging bullets to shoot Frenchmen. But she needed help. 'Help yourself,' she shrugged.

Helmut placed his gun carefully across a hay-bale. Thérèse saw how he had held it as if it was something he had found in his hands without knowing who had put it there or why. He removed his shirt and went over to the cow. His pale chest gleamed in the dim light. He murmured something in the cow's ear; something Thérèse couldn't understand so it sounded like a magic spell to her. The cow staggered to its feet.

'Bring the lamp closer,' he said. He examined the cow, all the time whispering in its ear, blowing in its nostrils. 'There are two calves and their limbs are tangled.' He thrust his arm into the birth canal and pushed and twisted inside. Thérèse stood by, feeling as soft and useless as Natalie, who had let her down.

It took an hour to coax the first calf out. Finally, it lay panting on the damp straw, weak, but alive. Helmut pushed it closer to its mother who began to lick its wet face. 'The other's not ready yet. We wait.'

'So, you live on a farm?' Thérèse asked awkwardly.

Helmut looked away. 'Yes. It was a good farm, once. The soil is dark and rich, not stony like here. The cow stirred and his mood suddenly changed. 'Quick. Quick. Put your arms round my waist. Yes, that's it. Now. Together. Pull!'

Thérèse wrapped her arms about his naked chest. She could smell his body, a rich mixture of sweat and good, rich earth. She watched as the snout of the calf emerged. She gripped Helmut more tightly in her excitement. But he had relaxed his hold on the rope as the calf slipped out with ease, still enveloped in its soft wet membrane. Down they both went, the bloody straw greasing their feet. They still clung together, rolling about, trying to regain their balance and dignity. As the soldier struggled to right himself, he almost flattened the flailing new-born.

Thérèse cried out a warning, 'No! No! Get off! Get off!'

There was a flash and a sharp explosion that shook the rafters. Something whistled past her ear and the boy slumped in her arms. Thérèse pulled herself up and stared at the man who had fired the shot. It was Thierry. Natalie was clinging to his shirt, screaming. Behind them an angry dawn slashed a blooded blade between the sky and the land.

'You fool!' Thérèse snarled at Natalie. 'You stupid, little fool.' She cradled Helmut's head in her arm. He stared back at her, a look of astonishment across his kind, dead eyes. Still Natalie screamed.

'Shut up or we're all dead.'

Too late. The doors swung wide open. A pack of Germans rushed in. Saw Helmut's mangled corpse and Thierry with his gun. Thérèse grabbed Natalie and pulled her down. Thierry was too slow. After he fell, the soldiers went on a rampage around the village. Anyone who was unfortunate enough to step out of their doors was shot. Bullets flew from building to building pock-marking the stone.

Old Monsieur Tapis pulls on his boots, picks up his gun from the table and strides out into the sunshine. He points his rifle up and through the dry stems. Once, Twice. Again. Again. A volley of shots rises higher than the tower of the church.

With them rise a cloud of starlings. Never had he seen so many together, Monsieur Tapis later tells anyone who will listen. A hundred, maybe two hundred erupt like a black volcano, darkening the sky into night before wheeling off in the wake of the gunshots.

They settle on the village roofs, on the telegraph wires, the walls, gravestones and washing lines. They jostle on their makeshift roosts, lifting and flapping their black wings, circling the sky, landing, taking off, uncertain, bewildered.

Thérèse wakes with a jolt. The sound of gunfire, the smell of blood and fear and hatred pounding through her old bones. She stands up unfolding like a rusty umbrella. Sees armed soldiers circling her, black as death. Sees Natalie awash with tears clinging to her dead love. 'He was helping me, you fool. He was a fine young man and you killed him. Slut! You killed my brother. You shamed us all.' She lifts her apron to her face and sobs.

Brigitte watches the starlings as they whirl about the old woman. She is not afraid of them, but the old woman is terrified. She is raving like a mad-woman.

She runs to her, places her small hand on her shoulder. 'See, Madame. They are only birds. They will not hurt you. Leave them and they will return to the fields.' And sure enough as Brigitte leads her back to her chair, the birds rise one by one and flap back to the maize. Soon they are filling their beaks once more. The church clock strikes. One. Two.

The village waits trembling between the past and the present.

The church clocks strikes again. One. Two.

Thérèse grunts. Afraid? Who says she's afraid? She begins to speak, but the child interrupts.

'Why does the church clock always strike twice?'

'It doesn't. Go away child and leave me in peace.'

'Well, well,' smiles Natalie, fluffing up her hair, as Brigitte later tells her about the birds and the old woman. 'So you met the old witch of Cailloux-Sainte-Cecile.'

'She looked so sad, Grandmaman.'

‘I tried to tell her. But she would never listen.’

‘Grandmaman?’

‘Yes, ma petite?’

‘Why does the church clock always strike twice?’

‘It leaves time for wrongs to be righted and mistakes forgiven.’

But Thérèse only ever hears the clock strike once. She picks up her chair and goes back inside her house, locking the door behind her.

A LOGICAL EXPLANATION

'But forty's young these days, Mum,' Helen said when Lynne was having one of my 'I'm past it' days.

She looked down at my shapeless skirt and Tee-shirt that had been through the wash one spin-cycle too many and said nothing.

Helen and Debbie were paying me one of their duty visits, both sprawled on my sofa leaving me the floor as Charlie was stretched out on the armchair, shedding hairs, his claws shredding the upholstery. Bless them, they both feel she needed 'taking out of herself' since the divorce. The first months were spent drinking her wine and eating her out of Pringles whilst they pontificated on the 'all men are a waste of space' debate. Since both of them still adored their father and were never without some member of the hated species somewhere in the background, she felt this was a bit rich.

It didn't last, of course.

They've now changed tactics. Their latest project is clearly 'let's get mum fixed up whether she wants it or not'.

This tactic started when they took her out for an outrageously expensive dinner. It was when they were all at that mellow stage, giggly and stuffed with profiteroles that Helen murmured oh-so-casually, 'By the way, Mum. I'm having a few friends round to my flat on Friday. Why don't you come along?'

Discreetly undoing the top button of her skirt, Lynne said, 'Your friends won't want an old wrinkly like me cramping their style.'

'Don't worry,' said Helen waving her glass, 'there'll be one or two people your own age.'

'And, you need to get out more, Mum,' confirmed Debbie, not altogether helpfully.

Afterwards, Lynne couldn't believe she'd fallen for that one. She could only blame herself when she'd found herself in Helen's flat, wedged between a sofa and bowl of avocado dip and the only person her own age in the room who just so happened to be male, who decided she needed to know the rules of crown-green bowling.

A few weeks later it was Debbie's turn. 'I've got a spare ticket for *Les Misérables*. Please come.'

'Not sure it's my sort of thing'

'You'll love it.'

'No.'

But again she was beaten into submission, only to find that Debbie had gone down with flu and had been replaced by a limp-wristed individual, carrying a box of soft-centres and a wilting bunch of lilies.

'I really thought you and Len would get on like a house on fire,' a miraculously-recovered Debbie sighed the next morning when Lynne phoned to complain.

'Why?'

'Well, because…'

'Because he's old and boring?'

'Don't be silly.'

Helen took up the challenge with a seeming never-ending supply of available candidates. Where did she find them? Rent-a-Grandad? 'But, Mum, this one's so right for you. Mature. Rich. Architect. Designed that precinct by the bus-station.'

'The one that looks like an abattoir? No thanks.'

'He's an animal-lover. Keeps budgerigars.'

'No.'

'And gerbils.'

'No.'

'Perhaps you're right.'

Eventually, the girls got the message and the matchmaking attempts ended. Lynne breathed a mental sigh of relief, took up watercolour-painting and got a job in the make-up department of her local Debenhams. She enjoyed it because her customers were women. Not that she was totally against meeting an eligible man. But she wasn't going out of her way to find one.

Peace at last. Every evening when she got home from work, she would pour herself one glass of chilled white wine, kick off her shoes, put her feet up on her new reclining armchair and check for phone messages. Most of her friends always seemed to forget she was a working woman and hadn't got out of the habit of phoning her during the day.

'You have three messages,' chirped the disembodied voice. Message one. Beep. 'Hi Mum. It's Helen. Fancy a girl's night out tomorrow? No ulterior motive. Honest.'

Message two. Beep. 'Debbie here. How's the job going? Any chance of free samples? Let's catch a meal and talk about it.'

It would seem the truce was over. They meant well but needed to be told enough was enough. She was about to tell them both so when the last message whirred into action. Beep. A male voice filled her ear. Gravelly enough to be intriguing but warm enough to be seductive and yet, so forlorn she felt her heart tighten. 'Why don't you ever pick up the phone? Why don't you return my calls? Please give me another chance. Please. I'll be in *The Grapes of Wrath* at half past eight tomorrow. Please be there. I need to talk to you. I love you so very much.' Click. End of messages.

Who the hell was he? Not a clue. She trawled through the metal database of 'men who were in love with her' only to find it empty, of course. Then it dawned on her. She didn't know this man from Adam. It was a mistake. In his distressed state, he'd misdialled and blurted out his misery to a total stranger.

Poor soul. The hard-hearted bitch didn't deserve him. Lynne could see her clearly. A size-eight-blonde who, even as he declared his misery, was slipping into five-inch Jimmy Choos and applying jammy lip-gloss in preparation for a date with another man. And tomorrow, there he'd be in *The Grapes of Wrath*, wherever or whatever that was, waiting for her to appear, lifting his head eagerly every time the door opened, only to lower it when it wasn't her, which it could never be because she hadn't got the message… So what? She plunged a fork into the film lid and slammed the pack of vegetarian moussaka into the microwave. After all, if he was stupid enough to dial the wrong number, that was his problem.

And then as she gazed upon the moussaka turning a stately dance behind the glass, she saw him again, tears blurring his vision. No wonder he'd got the wrong number. Divorce or no divorce, she still recognized a broken heart when it landed on her answer-phone.

The moussaka tasted of cardboard dunked in a 'rich sun-dried tomato sauce'. She found *Eastenders* even more depressing than usual and opted for a good book and an early night but couldn't sleep. She thumped her pillow. What on earth was she doing lying awake worrying about a stranger? She'd even looked up *The Grapes of Wrath* in the Yellow Pages for goodness sake. It was a wine-bar in South Street. Only a short bus ride away. It wouldn't take long. It couldn't do any harm. Could it?

Next morning, bleary-eyed and still undecided, she called Helen. Her daughter was not amused. 'Have you completely lost your marbles? He sounds a real loser. Can't even use a phone. You need to find a man who can look after you. Strong. Dependable.'

'I'm not after a date with him. I merely want to tell him what happened.'

Debbie was equally emphatic. 'Don't be stupid. He might be a psychopath.'

'He sounded sweet and loveable.'

'I bet they said that about the Hannibal Lector.'

Instead of putting her off, their words had the opposite effect. She'd show her daughters she could take care of herself. She wasn't some starry eyed teenager wearing rose-tinted spectacles.

The Grapes of Wrath turned out to be a dim and dingy cellar from which music of high decibels and low quality boomed forth. The tables were fashioned from old barrels and the seats were smaller barrels cut in half and upturned. The whole place was a hideous throw-back to the nineteen seventies, even down to Marc Bolan warbling in the background.

She took a deep breath and told herself she had to see it through. She checked her watch. Almost eight. All she had to do was find the man and explain. He might even buy her a drink to say thank you. They'd make an evening of it and then find they had a lot in common…

Kerchungg! It was that quintessentially comic TV moment where the background music screeches to a halt. The penny had dropped. What an idiot! The message left on her answering machine wasn't a mistake. It was a set-up. And Lynne knew who to blame. Helen and Debbie had lulled her into a false sense of security. They were at it again. And this time they thought they were being really clever. They knew she had a stubborn streak and that she always liked to do the opposite of what people expected. They'd set up the sting, pretended to put her off, knowing she'd be bound to trot along. She had to smile at their persistence. But she wasn't falling for it. No way.

She swung round and made for the exit.

What happened next wasn't entirely clear to her. She

must have collided with one of those heavy tables or skidded in a slick of spilt wine. Because there she was, seconds later, flat on her back. Even as she lay there, pain radiating from her wrist to her shoulder, she was aware of the corny nature of the situation. As a strong male arms gathered her up and placed her on one of the upturned barrels, she knew she he would be the right age, handsome and definitely not into crown-green bowling. He was tanned, slim, immaculately, but not over-immaculately, dressed in a pair of dark blue chinos and a beige shirt, casually unbuttoned at the neck. His hair was slightly greying at the temples and deep laughter lines framed his hazel eyes.

Not bad, girls. Not bad. And it may have been the bang on the head that allowed her to accept a glass of very expensive red wine from him. Not only that. She downed it so quickly that he immediately bought a bottle of rather luscious Cabernet Sauvignon and led her over to a quiet, secluded corner.

After her third glass any injury she might have sustained had melted away and the hideous wine bar miraculously transformed itself into a temple of delight. His name was Adam, divorced like her. He was an actor, currently appearing at the local theatre in the very production of *Les Misérables* she'd been forced to endure in the company of Len and his wilting lilies. As they swapped anecdotes, discussed the books and music they loved, chatted and laughed, the pieces began to fall into place. Helen or Debbie must have met him at a party somewhere, found out he was an actor and had concocted the plan. She knew exactly what they'd have said to him. 'Sound pathetic. She's very soft-hearted. We'll make sure she turns up. Give her a lovely evening. Dad's been a total plonker. Let her know there are still some decent men around.'

Only it hadn't worked totally according to their little plot, had it? He never got a chance to put his acting talent to the test before she literally fell at his feet. And yet, if he was acting, he was very convincing, so she decided to play along for a while.

All too soon, the flickering candles had melted to stubs. It seemed a shame to spoil what had been the most enjoyable evening she'd had in ages, but the time had come to tell him she wasn't fooled.

'So how did you know it was me when you picked me up from the floor?' she began cautiously. 'After all, there must be hundreds of middle-aged women with bags under their eyes and swollen ankles.'

'I beg your pardon?'

Perhaps she sounded more drunk to him than she did to herself. But she wasn't drunk. She'd only drunk three glasses, well, four, she supposed if she counted the first glass he bought her. She was high on happiness. She repeated the question with difficulty. 'Still not with you,' he said, frowning but still looking wonderful.

Maybe, she hoped, he was playing dumb because he liked her just that little bit, after all and wasn't ready to end the evening just yet. But Lynne couldn't live on dreams. She wanted things out in the open.

'I don't usually drink with strange men,' she explained. 'I only meant to give you the message and go home. Only there wasn't a message, was there? No size-eight-blonde nor a broken heart. You really are a brilliant actor.'

He looked anxious. 'Are you really sure you're all right? Perhaps he thought *she* was the psychopath or at least a pathetic case of post-divorce flakiness. 'I'd better get you home,' he said and get to the bottom of all this. I'm sure there's a logical explanation.'

Just then a bearded man in green tweed emerged from

another part of the bar she hadn't known was there. He pushed past them, muttering into his mobile. 'I've been here for hours,' he moaned. 'Perhaps you couldn't make it but you could have let me know. I'll be in *The Noble Rot* at eight tomorrow. Please be there.'

'There's an explanation all right,' she said, hooking her arm into Adam's, 'but I'm not sure it's at all logical.

ABOUT THE AUTHOR

Although Sally loved writing stories and reading novels from an early age, secondary school sent her in the wrong direction, away from scribbling stories and poems. She wrote nothing worth publishing until her two sons were in their teens. Her commercial fiction was published in *Women's Own, The Lady, Women's Weekly, The People's Friend* and *My Weekly* and won several prizes. She also submitted her literary short stories to Jo Derrick, the editor of *QWF (Quality Women's Fiction)*. Since then, they have remained firm friends, supporting each other, in tears and laughter ever since. Her historical novel *Hope Against Hope*, and novella *Chasing Angels*, are available to order in bookshops and online.

LIKE TO READ MORE WORK LIKE THIS?

Then sign up to our mailing list and download our free collection of short stories, *Magnetism*. Sign up now to receive this free e-book and also to find out about all of our new publications and offers.

Sign up here:
http://eepurl.com/gbpdVz

PLEASE LEAVE A REVIEW

Reviews are so important to writers. Please take the time to review this book. A couple of lines is fine.

Reviews help the book to become more visible to buyers. Retailers will promote books with multiple reviews.

This in turn helps us to sell more books… And then we can afford to publish more books like this one.

Leaving a review is very easy.

Go to https://amzn.to/48WVYiW, scroll down the left-hand side of the Amazon page and click on the 'Write a customer review' button.

OTHER WRITING BY SALLY ZIGMOND

Hope Against Hope

Published by Myrmidon Books Ltd.

Stoical and industrious Carrie and carefree and vivacious May lose both home and livelihood when their Leeds pub is sold out from under them to make way for the coming of the railway. They head for Harrogate to find work and lodging in the spa town s burgeoning hotel trade. But the sisters fall prey to fraudsters and predators and are also driven apart by misunderstanding, pride and a mutual sense of betrayal and resentment.

Alex Sinclair, a bold and warm-spirited Scot, has eschewed the wishes of his father to become a railway engineer. His companion, Charles Hammond is the dissolute heir to a vast fortune, withheld from him by an overbearing mother and grasping stepfather. Charles bides his time as a physician, a profession for which he lacks both aptitude and enthusiasm. The futures of both men will become bound up with those of the two sisters.

'A fabulous, humongous book that will take you through every emotion you own, and a few you'd forgotten you have.' (*Amazon*)

Order from Amazon:

Paperback: ISBN 978-1-905802-19-7
eBook: ASIN B004M18UUU

Chasing Angels

Published by Biscuit Publishing Ltd.

In 1794, Henriette d'Angeville was born into a French aristocratic family in crisis. Her grandfather was guillotined and her father imprisoned but later released causing the family to live on their memories in an impoverished château. In 1836, she was the first woman to reach the summit of Mont Blanc – in a bonnet and petticoats!

This novella is a fictional account of her life in which her love of the outdoors and her determination to excel in her climbing endeavours, which made her an object of derision and pity, is examined in a witty and sympathetic portrayal. We see her father, her mother and her younger brother. We see her at school and the circumstances in which she 'rescued' her companion, Jeannette, from destitution. We meet the Protestant ladies of Genevan society and the men of Chamonix who accompany her on her expedition.

'This may be a short book but what Sally Zigmond has written is a big story' (*Amazon*)

Order from Amazon:

Paperback: ISBN 978-1-903914-29-8
eBook: ASIN: B07XHL7CHS

OTHER PUBLICATIONS BY BRIDGE HOUSE

A Gentle Nudge

by Mason Bushell

Stories to soothe your soul.

In a world drowning in negativity and dark events, we all need a little light and hope. With a little adventure, romance and even music, these short stories will give your hopes and dreams a nudge as they draw a smile.

A Gentle Nudge by Mason Bushell wraps you in calm.

Order from Amazon:

Paperback: ISBN 978-1-914199-42-4
eBook: ISBN 978-1-914199-43-1

The Adventures of Iris and Zach

by I.L. Green

Iris and Zach have an uneasy but intriguing run.

A vast patchwork landscape of life is displayed through stories relating both the wonder and absurdity we all recognize. With a focus on mental health, these stories take the reader from incarceration to freedom, fear to comfort. There are celebrations of life and poetic lows. The Yin and Yang aspects of life are recognized in new and deliberate examples that instil thoughtfulness and occasionally a smile.

Order from Amazon:

Paperback: ISBN 978-1-914199-34-9
eBook: ISBN 978-1-914199-35-6

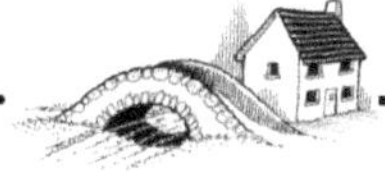

Weird Science

by Doug Hawley

Who would have thought it?

An abominable snowman speaks, dreams so good you'll never want to wake up, metaphysical questions, a cat with telepathy, a magical stream in USA's Northwest, and an unexpected invasion from the far north of Canada.

You will find all this and more in one book of Weird Science.

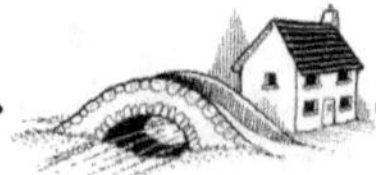

refuses to co-operate. Did I tell you my publisher telephoned me yesterday – actually telephoned – a thing never heard of from an old-fashioned gentleman such as him – with his copperplate script – asking when he could expect Millie's latest adventure? I'm keeping Hardcastle Brothers afloat single-handedly, as it is. I bluffed and blustered and said he wasn't to worry. That caused a stir in the boarding house over breakfast I can tell you. How they whispered over their bacon.

But, yes, I am worried about not writing. My mind is blank. Perhaps I should invite Lila here to explain why Percy is impossible, why he didn't telephone and what's that about a bank book (I can't decipher her scribbles.) Do you reckon Agnes has a Balkan lover who pilots an airship and she is waiting for him to appear in the sky to drop secret documents through her window? And what was the reason for Jack's silence for over three years? Was he in prison, the Foreign Legion, or prospecting for gold in Canada…?

Will Marchmont, you are a genius! That's it. Millie Wagstaff is off to the Yukon on the scent of a Balkan airship pilot who's stolen government secrets. Mr Hardcastle's going to be so pleased with me. I'd better get scribbling so I can finish this wretched novel before baby arrives – or the sea laps at my feet. Whichever is sooner.

www.ingramcontent.com/pod-product-compliance
Lightning Source LLC
LaVergne TN
LVHW010101110826
845155LV00028B/438

* 9 7 8 1 9 1 4 1 9 9 5 4 7 *